PENGUIN CLASSICS
Madame Maigret's Friend

'I love reading Simenon. He makes me think of Chekhov'
– William Faulkner

'A truly wonderful writer . . . marvellously readable – lucid, simple, absolutely in tune with the world he creates'
– Muriel Spark

'Few writers have ever conveyed with such a sure touch, the bleakness of human life'
– A. N. Wilson

'One of the greatest writers of the twentieth century . . . Simenon was unequalled at making us look inside, though the ability was masked by his brilliance at absorbing us obsessively in his stories'
– *Guardian*

'A novelist who entered his fictional world as if he were part of it'
– Peter Ackroyd

'The greatest of all, the most genuine novelist we have had in literature'
– André Gide

'Superb . . . The most addictive of writers . . . A unique teller of tales'
– *Observer*

'The mysteries of the human personality are revealed in all their disconcerting complexity'
– Anita Brookner

'A writer who, more than any other crime novelist, combined a high literary reputation with popular appeal'– P. D. James

'A supreme writer . . . Unforgettable vividness' – *Independent*

'Compelling, remorseless, brilliant'
– John Gray

'Extraordinary masterpieces of the twentieth century'
– John Banville

ABOUT THE AUTHOR

Georges Simenon was born on 12 February 1903 in Liège, Belgium, and died in 1989 in Lausanne, Switzerland, where he had lived for the latter part of his life. Between 1931 and 1972 he published seventy-five novels and twenty-eight short stories featuring Inspector Maigret.

Simenon always resisted identifying himself with his famous literary character, but acknowledged that they shared an important characteristic:

> My motto, to the extent that I have one, has been noted often enough, and I've always conformed to it. It's the one I've given to old Maigret, who resembles me in certain points . . . 'understand and judge not'.

Penguin is publishing the entire series of Maigret novels.

GEORGES SIMENON

Madame Maigret's Friend

Translated by HOWARD CURTIS

PENGUIN BOOKS

PENGUIN CLASSICS

UK | USA | Canada | Ireland | Australia
India | New Zealand | South Africa

Penguin Books is part of the Penguin Random House group of companies
whose addresses can be found at global.penguinrandomhouse.com.

First published in French as *L'amie de Mme Maigret* by Presses de la Cité 1950
This translation first published 2016

005

Typeset in Dante MT Std by Palimpsest Book Production Ltd, Falkirk, Stirlingshire

Printed and bound in Great Britain by Clays Ltd, Elcograf S.p.A.

ISBN: 978-0-241-24016-8

www.greenpenguin.co.uk

MIX
Paper from
responsible sources
FSC® C018179
www.fsc.org

Penguin Random House is committed to a
sustainable future for our business, our readers
and our planet. This book is made from Forest
Stewardship Council® certified paper.

Contents

Contents

1. *The Young Woman in Square d'Anvers*

The chicken was on the stove, along with a fine red carrot, a big onion and a bunch of parsley, the ends sticking out of the pan. Madame Maigret leaned down and checked that the gas, which was on a very low flame, wasn't likely to go out. Then she closed the windows, except for the one in the bedroom, asked herself if she'd forgotten anything, glanced at herself in the mirror and, satisfied, left the apartment, locked the door behind her and put the key in her bag.

It was just after ten on a March morning. The air was crisp, with a sparkling sun over Paris. She could have walked to Place de la République and caught a bus to Boulevard Barbès, which would have got her to Place d'Anvers in plenty of time for her eleven o'clock appointment.

But because of the young woman, she walked down the steps into the Richard-Lenoir Métro station, which was very close to home, and made the whole journey underground, looking out with half an eye, whenever they pulled into a station, at the familiar posters on the cream-coloured walls.

Maigret had teased her about it, but not too much, because, for the past three weeks, he'd had a lot on his mind.

'Are you sure there isn't a good dentist closer to home?'

Madame Maigret had never before had to have her teeth seen to. It was Madame Roblin, the lady with the dog who lived on the fourth floor of their apartment building, who had told her so much about Dr Floresco that she had decided to go and see him.

'He has fingers like a pianist. You don't even feel him working on your mouth. And if you tell him I sent you, he'll only charge you half price.'

He was a Romanian, who had his surgery on the third floor of a building at the corner of Rue Turgot and Avenue Trudaine, just facing Square d'Anvers, the park in Place d'Anvers. Was this Madame Maigret's seventh or eighth visit? The appointment was always for eleven o'clock. It had become a routine.

The first day, because of her obsessive fear of keeping people waiting, she'd arrived a good fifteen minutes ahead of time and had twiddled her thumbs in a room overheated by a gas stove. On her second visit, she'd also had to wait. Both times, she hadn't been admitted to the surgery until a quarter past eleven.

When it came to her third appointment, because the sun was shining and the park opposite was alive with birdsong, she had decided to go and sit on a bench and wait until it was time for her to see the dentist. That was how she had made the acquaintance of the woman with the little boy.

By now, it had become so much a habit that she deliberately left home early and took the Métro in order to have more time.

It was pleasant to look at the grass and the buds already half open on the branches of the few trees, which stood out against the wall of the secondary school. Sitting there on the bench in the sun, you could see the bustle of Boulevard Rochechouart, the green and white buses looking like big animals, the taxis weaving in and out.

The woman was there, just as on the other mornings, in her blue tailored suit and that little white hat that looked so fetching on her and was so springlike. She shifted on the bench to make room for Madame Maigret, who had brought a bar of chocolate and now held it out to the child.

'Say thank you, Charles.'

He was two years old, and what was most striking about him were his big dark eyes, with huge lashes that made him look like a girl. At first, Madame Maigret had wondered if he was talking, if the syllables he uttered actually belonged to a language. Then she had realized, without daring to ask their nationality, that he and the woman were foreigners.

'As far as I'm concerned,' Madame Maigret said, 'March is still the loveliest month in Paris, in spite of the showers. Some prefer May or June, but everything's so fresh in March.'

From time to time she would turn to look at the dentist's windows, because, from where she sat, she could just about see the head of the patient who usually went before her. He was a rather grumpy man in his fifties who was gradually having all his teeth extracted. She had made his acquaintance, too. He was originally from Dunkirk and lived locally with his married daughter, although he didn't like his son-in-law.

This morning, the little boy had a small red bucket and a spade and was playing with the gravel. He was always very clean, very well turned out.

'I think I'm only going to need another two visits,' Madame Maigret sighed. 'Dr Floresco told me he's going to start on the last tooth today.'

The woman smiled as she listened. She spoke excellent French, with a hint of an accent that made it all the more charming. At six or seven minutes to eleven, she was still smiling at the boy, who was quite surprised at the dust he had sent up into his own face, then all at once seemed to look at something in Avenue Trudaine, appeared to hesitate, then stood up and said quickly, 'Would you mind keeping an eye on him for a minute? I'll be right back.'

In the heat of the moment Madame Maigret wasn't too surprised, although she hoped, thinking of her appointment, that the woman would come back in time. Tactfully, she didn't turn to see where she was going.

The boy hadn't noticed anything. He was squatting, still playing at filling his red bucket with pebbles, then overturning it and untiringly starting all over again.

Madame Maigret didn't have the time on her. Her watch hadn't been working for years, and she never thought of taking it to the watchmaker. An old man came and sat down on the bench. He must be a local, because she'd seen him before.

'Would you be so kind as to tell me the time, monsieur?'

He couldn't have had a watch either, because he simply replied, 'About eleven.'

You couldn't see anybody's head now in the dentist's

window. Madame Maigret was starting to get worried. She felt ashamed of keeping Dr Floresco waiting: he was so gentle, so nice, and always so very patient.

She looked around the square, but there was no sign of the young lady in the white hat. Had she suddenly been taken ill? Or had she spotted someone she needed to talk to?

A policeman was crossing the park, and Madame Maigret stood up to ask him the time. It was indeed eleven o'clock.

The woman hadn't returned and the minutes were passing. The boy had looked up at the bench and seen that his mother wasn't there any more, but hadn't appeared to be worried.

If only Madame Maigret could let the dentist know! There was only the street to cross, and three floors to climb. She almost asked the old man in her turn to keep an eye on the boy, long enough for her to go and inform Dr Floresco, but she didn't dare, just stood there looking around her with growing impatience.

The second time she asked a passer-by for the time it was half past eleven. The old man had gone. She was the only person on the bench. She had seen the patient who came before her leave the building on the corner and set off in the direction of Rue Rochechouart.

What should she do? Had something happened to the woman? If she'd been run over by a car, a crowd would have gathered, people would have come running. Was the boy going to start panicking now?

It was a ridiculous situation. Maigret would tease her

even more than before. She would telephone the dentist later to apologize. Would she dare tell him what had happened?

She felt hot suddenly, because her nervousness made her skin flush. 'What's your name?' she asked the boy.

But he simply looked at her with his dark eyes and said nothing.

'Do you know where you live?'

He wasn't listening to her. It had already occurred to Madame Maigret that he didn't understand French.

'Excuse me, monsieur. Could you tell me the time, please?'

'Twenty-two minutes to twelve, madame.'

The woman still had not returned. Nor was she there by midday, when factory sirens screamed in the neighbourhood and stonemasons invaded a nearby bar.

Dr Floresco left the building and got into a small black car, but Madame Maigret didn't dare leave the boy to go and apologize.

What worried her now was her chicken, which was still on the stove. Maigret had told her it was more than likely that he would be back for lunch at about one o'clock.

Should she inform the police? To do that, she would have to leave the park. If she took the child with her and his mother returned in the meantime, she would go mad with worry. Then God knows where would she run to, and where they would meet up again! But she couldn't just leave a two-year-old alone in the middle of the park, so close to where all the buses and cars were endlessly passing.

'Excuse me, monsieur, could you tell me what time it is?'

'Half past twelve.'

The chicken must be starting to burn by now, and Maigret was on his way home. It would be the first time, in all these years of marriage, that he wouldn't find her there.

Phoning him was impossible too, because she would have to leave the park and go to a bar. If only she could see the policeman who'd passed earlier, or another policeman, she'd say who she was and ask him to kindly telephone her husband. As if on purpose, there wasn't a single policeman in sight. She looked in all directions, sat down, stood up again. She kept thinking she caught a glimpse of the white hat, but it was never the one she was waiting for.

She counted more than twenty white hats in half an hour, and four of them were worn by young women in blue tailored suits.

At eleven o'clock, while Madame Maigret was starting to get worried, forced to wait in the middle of a park looking after a child whose name she didn't even know, Maigret was putting his hat on his head, leaving his office, saying a few words to Lucas and heading grouchily towards the little door that leads from the headquarters of the Police Judiciaire to the Palais de Justice.

It had become a routine, pretty much for the same period of time that Madame Maigret had been going to see the dentist in the 9th arrondissement. Maigret came to the corridor where the examining magistrates had their offices, and where there were always strange characters waiting on benches, some surrounded by two gendarmes, and knocked on the door that bore Judge Dossin's name.

'Come in.'

Judge Dossin was the tallest examining magistrate in Paris, and he always seemed embarrassed by his size, always seemed to be apologizing for having the aristocratic figure of a borzoi.

'Sit down, Maigret. Smoke your pipe. Did you read this morning's article?'

'I haven't seen the papers yet.'

The judge pushed one towards him. It had a big headline on the front page:

THE STEUVELS CASE
Maître Philippe Liotard addresses
the League for Human Rights

'I had a long conversation with the prosecutor,' Dossin said. 'He's of the same opinion as myself. We couldn't release the bookbinder even if we wanted to, not while Liotard is still kicking up such a fuss.'

A few weeks earlier, that name had been more or less unknown at the Palais de Justice. Philippe Liotard, who was barely thirty, had never pleaded a major case. After five years as one of the secretaries of a famous lawyer, he was only just starting out on his own and was still living in an unglamorous bachelor apartment in Rue Bergère, next door to a brothel.

But now, since the Steuvels case had come to light, he

was never out of the newspapers, was constantly giving interviews that caused a stir, issuing statements, even appearing in newsreels, with tousled hair and a sarcastic smile on his lips.

'Anything new on your side?'

'Nothing worth mentioning, your honour.'

'Are you still hoping to track down the man who left the telegram?'

'Torrence is in Concarneau. He's smart.'

In the three weeks that it had been grabbing public attention, the Steuvels case had generated some interesting headlines, like the chapter headings of a serialized novel.

It had started with:

The cellar in Rue de Turenne

As luck would have it, this was an area that Maigret knew well, had even dreamed of living in, less than fifty metres from Place des Vosges.

Leaving the narrow Rue des Francs-Bourgeois at the corner of the square, and going up Rue de Turenne towards the République, the first thing you see on your left-hand side is a bistro, painted yellow, then a dairy, the Salmon dairy. Next door is a workshop with a low ceiling and a dusty front window on which you can read in faded letters: Master Bookbinder. In the shop after that, the widow Rancé sells umbrellas.

Between the workshop and the umbrella shop there is an arched carriage entrance with a concierge's lodge and, at the far end of the courtyard, a former town-house, now swarming with offices and apartments.

A corpse in the stove?

What the public did not know, and the police had taken care not to tell the press, was that the case had come to light by pure chance. One morning, a dirty scrap of wrapping paper had been found in the letterbox of the Police Judiciaire on Quai des Orfèvres. It bore the words:

The bookbinder in Rue de Turenne has been
burning a body in his stove.

It wasn't signed, of course. The paper had ended up on Maigret's desk. Treating it with scepticism, he hadn't disturbed any of his older inspectors with it, but had sent young Lapointe, who was dying to make a name for himself.

Lapointe had discovered that there was indeed a bookbinder in Rue de Turenne. His name was Frans Steuvels, and he was a Belgian from Flanders who had been living in France for more than twenty-five years. Passing himself off as an employee of the sanitary department, Lapointe had inspected the premises and had come back with a detailed floor plan.

'Basically, sir, Steuvels works in the window. The workshop goes back a long way, and gets darker the further you get from the street. It's divided by a wooden partition, and Steuvels and his wife have their bedroom behind that.

'There's a staircase leading down to the basement. That's where the kitchen is, then a little room where the light has to be kept on all day long and which they use as a dining room, and finally a cellar.'

'With a stove?'

'Yes. An old model, which doesn't seem to be in a particularly good state.'

'In working order?'

'It wasn't on this morning.'

It was Sergeant Lucas who had gone back to Rue de Turenne for an official search at about five that afternoon. Fortunately, he had taken the precaution of taking a warrant with him, because the bookbinder had refused at first to let him search.

Lucas had come close to leaving empty-handed. Now that the case had become a nightmare for the Police Judiciaire, he was almost resented for having eventually found something after all.

Sifting through the ashes at the very bottom of the stove, he had come across two teeth, two human teeth, which he had immediately taken to the laboratory.

'What kind of man is this bookbinder?' Maigret had asked: at that moment he was still only dealing with the case from a distance.

'He must be about forty-five. He has red hair, pock-marked skin and blue eyes. He's very mild-mannered. His wife, who's much younger than him, watches over him like a child.'

By now it was known that Fernande, who had become famous in her own right, had arrived in Paris as a domestic and had then spent several years as a streetwalker in the Boulevard de Sébastopol area.

She was thirty-six and had been living with Steuvels for ten years. Three years earlier, for no apparent reason, they had got married at the town hall of the 3rd arrondissement.

The laboratory had sent its report. The teeth were those of a man of about thirty, probably quite well-built, who must still have been alive a few days earlier.

Steuvels had been brought to Maigret's office, and the 'singing session' had begun. He had sat in the armchair with the green velvet upholstery, facing the window that looked out on the Seine. It had been raining heavily that evening. For the ten or twelve hours that the interrogation had lasted, rain could be heard beating against the windowpanes, and water gurgled in the gutter. Steuvels wore steel-rimmed glasses with thick lenses. His long hair was dishevelled and his tie was askew.

He was a cultivated, well-read man. He was calm, thought everything over carefully, and his fine gingery skin became easily inflamed.

'How do you explain the fact that human teeth were found in your stove?'

'I can't.'

'You haven't lost any teeth lately? Or your wife?'

'Neither of us. Mine are false.'

He had removed his dentures from his mouth, then put them back with a casual gesture.

'Can you tell me how you spent your time on the evenings of 16th, 17th and 18th February?'

The interrogation had taken place on the evening of the 21st, after the visits of Lapointe and Lucas to Rue de Turenne.

'Is one of those days a Friday?'

'The 16th.'

'In that case, I went to the Saint-Paul cinema in Rue Saint-Antoine. I go there every Friday.'

'With your wife?'

'Yes.'

'And the other two days?'

'Fernande left on Saturday morning.'

'Where did she go?'

'To Concarneau.'

'Had the trip been planned for a long time?'

'Her mother, who's disabled, lives with her daughter and son-in-law in Concarneau. On Saturday morning, we got a telegram from the sister, Louise, saying that their mother was seriously ill, and Fernande caught the first train.'

'Without phoning first?'

'They don't have a phone.'

'Was the mother very ill?'

'She wasn't ill at all. The telegram wasn't from Louise.'

'Who was it from, then?'

'We don't know.'

'Have you ever been a victim of that kind of hoax before?'

'No, never.'

'When did your wife get back?'

'On Tuesday. She took advantage of being there to spend a couple of days with her family.'

'What did you do during that time?'

'I worked.'

'A neighbour claims that thick smoke was coming out of your chimney on Sunday.'

'It's possible. It was cold.'

That was true. Sunday and Monday had been very cold, and there had even been severe frost reported in the suburbs.

'What clothes were you wearing on Saturday evening?'

'The same ones I'm wearing now.'

'Nobody came to see you after you closed up?'

'Nobody, except for a customer who came to collect a book. Do you want his name and address?'

He was a well-known man, a member of the Cent Bibliophiles. Thanks to Liotard, they were going to hear a lot about this association, most of whose members were important figures.

'Your concierge, Madame Salazar, heard someone knocking at your door at about nine o'clock that evening. Several people were having an animated conversation.'

'People talking on the pavement outside maybe, not inside. Though if they were as animated as Madame Salazar claims, they may well have knocked against the shopfront.'

'How many suits do you own?'

'Just as I only have one body and one head, I only own one suit and one hat, apart from the old trousers and jumper I wear for work.'

He had then been shown a navy-blue suit found in the wardrobe in his bedroom.

'What about this?'

'It's not mine.'

'Then how come this suit was found in your wardrobe?'

'I've never seen it before. Anybody could have put it there in my absence. I've been here for six hours now.'

'Would you mind putting on the jacket?'

It fitted him.

'Do you see these stains, which look like rust stains? It's blood, human blood, according to the experts. Someone tried to rub them off, but couldn't.'

'I don't know this jacket.'

'Madame Rancé, who owns the umbrella shop, says she's often seen you in blue, especially on Fridays, when you go to the cinema.'

'I used to have another suit, which was blue, but I got rid of it more than two months ago.'

After this first interrogation, Maigret was morose. He had had a long conversation with Judge Dossin, after which both had gone to see the prosecutor.

It was the latter who had taken responsibility for the arrest.

'The experts agree, don't they? The rest is up to you, Maigret. Go ahead. We can't release this fellow.'

The very next day Maître Liotard had emerged from the shadows, and ever since he'd been snapping at Maigret's heels like a vicious little dog.

Among the headlines in the newspapers, there was one that had caught on:

The Phantom Suitcase

Young Lapointe claimed that when he had visited the premises, pretending to be an employee of the sanitary department, he had seen a reddish-brown suitcase under a table in the workshop.

'It was an ordinary, cheap suitcase. I knocked into it by accident. I was surprised that it hurt so much, and I understood why when I tried to move it, because it was unusually heavy.'

But by five that afternoon, when Lucas did his search, the suitcase was gone. More precisely, there was still a suitcase there, also brown, also cheap, but Lapointe asserted that it wasn't the same one.

'It's the suitcase I took with me to Concarneau,' Fernande had said. 'We've never owned another. We almost never travel.'

Lapointe insisted it wasn't the same suitcase: the first one had been lighter in colour, and its handle had been repaired with string.

'If I'd had a suitcase to repair,' Steuvels had retorted, 'I would never have used string. Don't forget I'm a bookbinder. I work with leather all the time.'

At this point, Philippe Liotard had sought testimonials from bibliophiles, and it had emerged that Steuvels was one of the best bookbinders in Paris, perhaps the best, to whom collectors entrusted their most delicate tasks, particularly the refurbishment of old bindings.

Everyone agreed that he was a quiet man who spent almost all his time in his workshop, and although the police searched in his past for something dubious, they failed to find anything.

Of course, there was the business of Fernande. He had met her when she was still on the streets, and it was he who had taken her away from that life. But that was all a long time ago, and there had been nothing against Fernande since then either.

Torrence had been in Concarneau for four days. At the post office, they had found the original of the telegram, written by hand in capital letters. The postmistress thought she remembered that it was a woman who had handed it in, and Torrence was still searching, drawing up a list of travellers who had recently arrived from Paris, questioning two hundred people a day.

'We've had enough of Detective Chief Inspector Maigret's so-called infallibility!' Maître Liotard had declared to a reporter.

And he brought up the fact that there were by-elections coming up in the 3rd arrondissement, which might well have led certain people to start a scandal in the neighbourhood for political ends.

Judge Dossin was also hauled over the coals, and these attacks, which weren't always subtle, upset him a great deal.

'So you don't have the slightest new lead?'

'I'm still looking. There are ten of us looking, sometimes more. We've questioned some people twenty times by now. Lucas is hoping to track down the tailor who made the blue suit.'

As always when the public becomes fascinated by a case, they were receiving hundreds of letters daily. Almost all of them led nowhere and proved to be a waste of time.

But everything was scrupulously checked, and they even listened to people who were clearly mad but who claimed to know something.

At ten to one, Maigret got off the bus at the corner of Boulevard Voltaire, glanced up at the windows of his apartment as he usually did, and was slightly surprised to see that, in spite of the bright sun hitting it full on, the dining room window was closed.

He climbed the staircase laboriously and turned the handle of the door, which didn't open. Madame Maigret did sometimes lock the door when she was getting dressed or undressed. He opened it with his own key, found himself surrounded by a cloud of blue smoke and rushed to the kitchen to turn off the gas. In the saucepan, the chicken, the carrot and the onion were nothing but a black crust.

He opened all the windows, and when Madame Maigret opened the door half an hour later, out of breath, she found him sitting in front of a hunk of bread and a piece of cheese.

'What time is it?'

'Half past one,' he said calmly.

He had never seen her in such a state, her hat knocked sideways, her lips trembling.

'Please don't laugh.'

'I'm not laughing.'

'And don't tell me off. It was the only thing I could do, and I'd have liked to see you in my place. When I think you're eating a piece of cheese for lunch!'

'Was it the dentist?'

'I didn't see the dentist. I've been stuck in Square d'Anvers since a quarter to eleven, unable to move.'

'Were you taken ill?'

'Have I ever been ill in my life? No. It's because of the boy. By the time he started crying and stamping his feet, I was looking at people as if I was a thief.'

'What boy?'

'I told you about the woman in blue and her child, but you never listen to me. The one I met on the bench while I was waiting to see the dentist. This morning, she got up in a hurry, asked me to keep an eye on the boy for a moment and left.'

'And she didn't come back? What did you do with the boy?'

'She did come back in the end, just a quarter of an hour ago. I had to take a taxi here.'

'What did she tell you when she got back?'

'The amazing thing is she didn't tell me anything. I was in the middle of the park, stuck there like a weathervane, with the boy screaming loudly enough to alert passers-by.

'At last I saw a taxi stop at the corner of Avenue Trudaine and I recognized the white hat. She didn't even take the trouble to get out. She half opened the door and signalled to me. The boy ran ahead of me, and I was afraid he'd get run over. He got to the taxi first, and the door was already closing by the time I reached it.

'"Tomorrow," she called out. "I'll explain tomorrow. Forgive me . . ."

'She didn't say thank you. The taxi was already moving

off in the direction of Boulevard Rochechouart, and it turned left towards Pigalle.'

She fell silent, still out of breath. She took off her hat with such a brusque gesture that it messed up her hair.

'Are you laughing?'

'Of course not.'

'Admit it, it makes you laugh. The fact remains, she left her child with a stranger for more than two hours. She doesn't even know my name.'

'What about you? Do you know hers?'

'No.'

'Do you know where she lives?'

'I don't know anything at all, except that I missed my appointment, my lovely chicken is burnt, and you're eating cheese at the end of the table like a . . . like a . . .'

Then, not finding the word, she started crying and headed for the bedroom to change her clothes.

2. The Problems of the Grand Turenne

Maigret had his very own way of climbing the two floors of the Quai des Orfèvres: at the bottom of the staircase, where the light came in from outside in an almost pure state, he still seemed relatively nonchalant, but the more he penetrated the greyness of the old building, the more anxious he appeared, as if the worries of the office impregnated him the closer he got to them.

By the time he passed the clerk, he was already the chief. Lately, whether it was morning or afternoon, he had got into the habit, before opening his own door, of dropping into the inspectors' office and, still in his hat and coat, entering the 'Grand Turenne'.

This was the new refrain at the Quai, and revealed the significance the Steuvels case had assumed. Lucas, who had been entrusted with the task of centralizing information, collating it and keeping it up to date, had soon been overwhelmed, because he was also the one who answered telephone calls, looked through mail concerning the case and received informers.

Unable to work in the inspectors' office, where there were constant comings and goings, he had taken refuge in an adjacent room, on the door of which a mischievous hand had lost no time in writing: The Grand Turenne.

As soon as an inspector had finished with some other

case, or as soon as anyone came back from an assignment, a colleague would ask him, 'Are you free?'

'Yes.'

'Then go and see the Grand Turenne! He's hiring!'

It was true. Poor Lucas never had enough people to check things for him, and there was probably nobody left in the department who hadn't taken at least one turn in Rue de Turenne.

They all knew the crossroads near the bookbinder's, with its three cafés: first of all the café-restaurant on the corner of Rue des Francs-Bourgeois, then the Grand Turenne, opposite, and finally, thirty metres away, on the corner of Place des Vosges, the Tabac des Vosges, which the reporters had adopted as their headquarters, because they were also on the case.

The police, though, drank at the Grand Turenne, through the windows of which they could see Steuvels' workshop. That was their headquarters, of which Lucas' office had become a kind of branch.

The most surprising thing was that good old Lucas, spending all day in the office, was probably the only one who hadn't yet set foot in the bookbinder's since his first visit.

And yet, of all of them, it was he who knew the area best. He knew that after the Grand Turenne (the café!) there was a shop selling fine wines, the Caves de Bourgogne, and he knew the owners. He only had to consult a file to see what answers they had given.

No. They hadn't seen anything. But on Saturday evening, they had left for the Chevreuse Valley, where they spent the weekend in the house they'd had built.

After the Caves de Bourgogne came the cobbler's shop, owned by a Monsieur Bousquet.

He was quite different: he talked too much, but his great fault was that he didn't tell everyone the same thing. It depended on what time of day he was questioned and the number of aperitifs and little drinks he'd had at one of the three cafés, it didn't matter which one.

Then there was the Frère stationer's, a retail-wholesale business, and, in the courtyard behind, a cardboard factory.

Above Frans Steuvels' workshop, on the first floor of the former mansion, was a factory making cheap jewellery. This was the firm of Sass and Lapinsky, which employed some twenty female workers and four or five male workers with impossible names.

Everyone had been questioned, some of them four or five times, by different inspectors, not to mention all the reporters. Two white wooden tables in Lucas' office were covered in papers, maps and checklists, and he was the only one who could find anything in all that jumble.

Tirelessly, Lucas would update his notes. This afternoon, too, Maigret came and stood behind him without saying anything, puffing gently on his pipe.

A page headed 'Motives' was covered in notes which had been crossed out one after the other.

They had looked for a political angle. Not the one mentioned by Maître Liotard, because that didn't stand up. But Steuvels, who lived a solitary life, might have belonged to some subversive organization.

They hadn't found anything. The more they looked into his life, the more uneventful they realized it was. The books in his library, examined one by one, were by some of the greatest writers in the world, chosen by an intelligent and unusually cultivated man. Not only had he read and reread them, he had made annotations in the margin.

Could it have been jealousy? Fernande never went out without him, except to do her shopping in the neighbourhood, and from where he sat he could see almost everything she did in the shops where she bought her supplies.

They had wondered if there might be a connection between the supposed murder and the proximity of Sass and Lapinsky. Nothing had been stolen from the jeweller's. Neither the bosses nor the workers knew the bookbinder, except for having seen him in his window.

There was nothing from Belgium either. Steuvels had left at the age of eighteen and had never gone back. He wasn't involved in politics and there was nothing to suggest that he belonged to any kind of Flemish extremist movement.

Everything had been considered. Just to be on the safe side, Lucas accepted the craziest suggestions and would open the door of the inspectors' office and call someone at random.

They knew what that meant. A new check to be made, in Rue de Turenne or elsewhere.

'I may have something,' he said now to Maigret, pulling a sheet of paper from the scattered files. 'I had a call put out to all the taxi-drivers. This came in, from a naturalized Russian. I'll have it checked.'

That was the fashionable word. Things had to be checked!

'I wanted to know if a taxi had driven anyone to the bookbinder's on the evening of Saturday, February 17th. The driver, whose name is Georges Peskine, was hailed by three men near Gare Saint-Lazare at about 8.15 that Saturday, and asked to be driven to the corner of Rue de Turenne and Rue des Francs-Bourgeois. So it was after 8.30 when he dropped them, which would confirm the concierge's statement about the noises she heard. The driver doesn't know his passengers. But he says that the one who seemed to be the leader, the one who spoke to him, looked Middle Eastern.'

'What language did they use among themselves?'

'French. One of the other men, a tall fair-haired man, quite stout, in his thirties, with a strong Hungarian accent, seemed worried, ill at ease. The third man was a middle-aged Frenchman, less well-dressed than his companions, who didn't seem to belong to the same social circles.

'When they got out, the Middle Eastern man paid, and all three walked up Rue de Turenne in the direction of the bookbinder's.'

Without this story of the taxi, Maigret might not have thought of his wife's adventure.

'While you're dealing with taxi-drivers, you might perhaps try to find out about something that happened this morning. It has nothing to do with our case, but it intrigues me.'

Lucas might not be so convinced that it had nothing to do with his case, because he was ready to connect the most remote and fortuitous events to it. As soon as he arrived in the morning, he would get in all the reports from local police stations to make sure they contained nothing that might be linked to his sphere of activity.

Alone in his office, he was performing an enormous task, one which the public, reading the newspapers and following the Steuvels case as if it were a serial, were far from suspecting.

In a few words, Maigret told him the story of the woman in the white hat and the little boy.

'You might also phone the police in the 9th arrondissement. The fact that she was on the same bench in Square d'Anvers every morning suggests she lives locally. Maybe they can check the shops, hotels and apartment houses in the area.'

More checking! You would normally find up to ten inspectors at a time in the next office, smoking, writing reports, reading the papers or even playing cards. Now, it was rare to see two at the same time. No sooner had they come in than the Grand Turenne would open its doors.

'Are you free? Come here a minute.'

And another one would be sent to check out a lead.

They had looked for the missing suitcase in the left-luggage offices of all the stations and in all the second-hand shops.

Lapointe may have been inexperienced, but he was a conscientious young man, and he couldn't have made it up.

That meant that there had indeed been a suitcase in Steuvels' workshop on the morning of 21 February, a suitcase that was no longer there by the time Lucas had arrived at five o'clock.

As far as the neighbours could remember, Steuvels

hadn't left his home that day, and nobody had seen Fernande leave with a suitcase or a package.

Had anybody come to take delivery of bound books? That too had been 'checked'. The Argentine embassy had sent for a document for which Steuvels had produced a sumptuous binding, but it wasn't large and the courier had come out with it under his arm.

Martin, the most cultured man in the Police Judiciaire, had spent nearly a week in the bookbinder's workshop, studying the jobs he had done over the past few months, contacting customers by phone.

'He's an amazing man,' he had concluded. 'He has the most select clientele you can imagine. Everybody has complete confidence in him. He even works for quite a few embassies.'

But there was nothing mysterious about that either. The reason embassies entrusted him with work was that he was a heraldist and had the stamps for a large number of coats of arms, which allowed him to put the arms of various countries on the books or documents he bound.

'You don't look happy, chief. Something will come out of all this in the end, you'll see.'

And good old Lucas, who hadn't lost heart, pointed to the hundreds of papers he was cheerfully amassing.

'We found teeth in the stove, didn't we? They didn't get there by themselves. And someone did send a telegram from Concarneau to get Steuvels' wife there. The blue suit hanging in the wardrobe had human bloodstains someone had tried to get rid of. Whatever Maître Liotard might say or do, I can't get past that.'

But all that paperwork, with which Lucas was so intoxicated, depressed Maigret, who looked at it glumly.

'What are you thinking about, chief?'

'Nothing. I'm wondering.'

'About letting him go?'

'No. That's up to the examining magistrate.'

'If it wasn't, would you let him go?'

'I don't know. I'm wondering whether to start all over from the beginning.'

'That's up to you,' Lucas replied, somewhat hurt.

'That doesn't stop you carrying on with your work. On the contrary, if we delay too long we'll never find our way again. It's always the same: once the press get involved, everybody has something to say and we're submerged.'

'All the same, I found the driver, just as I'll find Madame Maigret's.'

Maigret filled another pipe and opened the door. There wasn't a single inspector next door. They were all out somewhere, dealing with the Steuvels case.

'Have you made up your mind?'

'I think so.'

He didn't even go into his office. He left Quai des Orfèvres and immediately hailed a taxi.

'The corner of Rue de Turenne and Rue des Francs-Bourgeois!'

Words that had been heard so often, from morning to night, they had become loathsome.

The locals had never had it so good. All of them had had their names in the papers at one time or another. Shopkeepers and artisans just had to drop by the Grand Turenne for a drink to bump into policemen and, if they crossed the street to the Tabac des Vosges, where the white wine was famous, the reporters were there to greet them.

Ten, twenty times, they had been asked what they thought of Steuvels and Fernande, and what details they could give about their doings.

As there wasn't even a corpse, when it came down to it, but only two teeth, there was no sense of tragedy. It was more of a game.

Maigret got out of the taxi outside the Grand Turenne, glanced inside, didn't see any of his men, walked a few steps and found himself in front of Steuvels' workshop, where, for the past three weeks, the shutters had been up and the door closed. There was no doorbell, and he knocked, sure that Fernande was at home.

It was in the morning that she went out. Every day since Frans had been arrested, she had left home at ten o'clock, carrying three small stacked saucepans held together by a hinge ending in a handle.

It was her husband's meal, which she took to him in the Santé prison, travelling there by Métro.

Maigret had to knock a second time, and saw her emerge from the stairs that joined the workshop and the basement. She recognized him, turned to speak to someone he couldn't see, and finally came and opened the door.

She was wearing a check apron and slippers. Seeing her like that, a little fatter now, no make-up on her face, no one would have recognized the woman who had once been a prostitute in the little streets around the Boulevard de Sébastopol. She looked every inch the conscientious housewife, and in normal times, she must have been good-humoured.

'Is it me you want to see?' she asked, not without a touch of weariness.

'Is there someone with you?'

As she didn't reply, Maigret went to the staircase, walked a little way down, leaned over and frowned.

He had already been told that Alfonsi was in the area, having an aperitif with the reporters in the Tabac des Vosges, but not setting foot in the Grand Turenne.

Now here he was, standing in the kitchen – where something was simmering on the stove – and looking for all the world like a regular. Embarrassed as he might have been, he gave Maigret an ironic smile.

'What are you doing here?'

'As you can see: paying a visit, like you. It's my right, isn't it?'

Alfonsi had been in the Police Judiciaire, although never in Maigret's team. For some years, he had worked in the vice squad, where he had finally been given to understand that in spite of his political contacts he was no longer wanted.

He was short, and in order to look taller wore built-up heels – some insinuated that he also put a pack of cards in his shoes. He always dressed in an excessively elegant manner, with a big diamond ring, which might have been real or fake, on his finger.

He had started a private detective agency in Rue Notre-Dame-de-Lorette, of which he was both boss and the one employee, assisted only by a woman who was less his secretary than his mistress, and with whom he was often seen in nightclubs.

When Maigret had been told of his presence in Rue de Turenne, he had thought at first that Alfonsi was trying to dig up the odd bit of information that he could then sell to the papers.

Then he had discovered that Philippe Liotard had hired him.

It was the first time he had run into him personally and he grunted, 'I'm waiting.'

'Waiting for what?'

'For you to go.'

'That's a pity, because I haven't finished.'

'As you wish.' Maigret pretended to head for the exit.

'What are you going to do?'

'Call one of my men and have him tail you day and night. That's my right too.'

'All right, I get the idea! No need to get nasty, Monsieur Maigret!'

He walked up the stairs, swaggering like a gangster and winking at Fernande as he left.

'Does he come here often?' Maigret asked.

'This is the second time.'

'I advise you not to trust him.'

'I know. I know those people.'

Was that a discreet allusion to the time when she had been dependent on the men in the vice squad?

'How's Steuvels?'

'Fine. He reads all day. He's confident.'

'What about you?'

Was there really a hesitation?

'So am I.'

All the same, it was obvious she was tired.

'What books are you taking him at the moment?'

'He's rereading Proust all the way through.'

'Have you also read Proust?'

'Yes.'

So Steuvels had educated the woman he had once picked up on the street.

'You're wrong to think of me as your enemy. You know the situation as well as I do. I want to understand. Right now, I don't understand any of it. Do you?'

'I'm sure Frans didn't commit any crime.'

'Do you love him?'

'The word doesn't mean anything. There ought to be another one, a word invented specially, but it doesn't exist yet.'

He had come back upstairs to the workshop where Steuvels' tools lay on the long table by the window. Behind, in the shadows, were the presses and on the shelves, books waiting their turn among others already started.

'He had regular habits, didn't he? I'd like you to give me his daily schedule, in as much detail as possible.'

'I've already been asked the same thing.'

'Who by?'

'Maître Liotard.'

'Did it ever occur to you that Maître Liotard's interests might not be the same as yours? Nobody knew who he was three weeks ago. He's trying to attract as much attention to himself as he can. He doesn't really care if your husband is innocent or guilty.'

'But if he proves that Frans is innocent, he'll get a lot of publicity and his reputation will be established.'

'What if he gets your husband released without actually proving his innocence? Everybody will say how clever he is. People will start going to him. And about your husband, they'll say, "He was lucky Liotard got him off!"'

'In other words, the guiltier Steuvels appears, the more credit Liotard will get. Do you understand that?'

'Frans understands it, and that's what matters.'

'Did he tell you that?'

'Yes.'

'Doesn't he like Liotard? Why did he choose him?'

'He didn't choose him. It was Liotard who—'

'Hold on a moment. You've just told me something important.'

'I know.'

'Did you do it deliberately?'

'Maybe. I'm tired of all this fuss about us and I know where it's coming from. I don't feel I'm hurting Frans by saying what I'm saying.'

'When Sergeant Lucas came to search the premises at about five o'clock on February 21st, he didn't leave on his own, but took your husband with him.'

'And you questioned him all night long,' she said reproachfully.

'It's my job. At that point, he didn't yet have a lawyer, since he didn't know he was going to be charged. And since then he's been in custody. He only came back here with some of my inspectors, and not for very long. But when I asked him to choose a lawyer, he gave me the name of Maître Liotard without any hesitation.'

'I see what you mean.'

'So did Liotard see Steuvels here before Sergeant Lucas came?'

'Yes.'

'In other words, on the afternoon of the 21st, between the visits by Inspector Lapointe and Sergeant Lucas?'

'Yes.'

'Were you present during their conversation?'

'No, I was downstairs doing the housework, because I'd been away for three days.'

'Do you know what they said to each other? Had they ever met before?'

'No.'

'Was it your husband who phoned him and asked him to come?'

'I'm pretty sure it was.'

Some kids from the neighbourhood came and stuck their faces to the window.

'Would you prefer it if we went downstairs?' Maigret suggested.

She led him across the kitchen to a little windowless room. It was very pretty and very intimate, with book-laden shelves all around, the table on which the couple ate and, in a corner, another table that served as a desk.

'You were asking me how my husband spent his time. He'd get up at six every day, winter or summer. In winter, the first thing he'd do would be to light the stove.'

'Why wasn't it lit on the 21st?'

'It wasn't cold enough. We'd had a few days of frost, but then the weather turned nice again. Neither of us feel the cold. In the kitchen, I have the gas oven which gives enough warmth, and there's another one in the workshop which Frans uses for his glue and his tools.

'Before washing, he'd go and get croissants from the bakery while I made the coffee, and we'd have our breakfast.

'Then he'd wash and get straight down to work. I'd leave the house around nine, with most of my housework finished, to go shopping.'

'He never went out to make deliveries?'

'Not very often. People would bring him work, and come and pick it up. When he had to deliver something, I'd go with him. That was more or less the only time we went out.

'We'd have lunch at 12.30.'

'Did he get back to work immediately after lunch?'

'He'd usually stand in the doorway for a while to have a cigarette. He never smoked while he was working.

'That would last until seven, sometimes half past. I never knew what time we'd eat, because he was determined to finish whatever work he had on. Then he'd put up the shutters, wash his hands, and after dinner we'd sit in this room and read until ten or eleven.

'Except for Friday evenings when we went to the Saint-Paul cinema.'

'Did he drink?'

'A glass of brandy every evening, after dinner. Just a

small glass, which lasted him a whole hour, because he only ever dipped his lips in it.'

'What about Sunday? Did you go to the country?'

'Never. He hated the country. We'd potter around all morning without getting dressed. He'd do odd jobs. He was the one who made the shelves and pretty much everything we have here. In the afternoon, we'd take a walk around the Francs-Bourgeois neighbourhood, then the Île Saint-Louis, and we often had dinner in a little restaurant near the Pont-Neuf.'

'Is he tight-fisted?'

She blushed. When she replied, it was more stiffly, and with a question, as is often the case when women are embarrassed. 'Why do you ask me that?'

'He's been working like this for more than twenty years, hasn't he?'

'He's worked all his life. His mother was very poor. He had an unhappy childhood.'

'And now he's apparently the most expensive book-binder in Paris. He doesn't have to tout for work, and even turns jobs down.'

'That's true.'

'With what he earns, you could have a comfortable life, a modern apartment, even a car.'

'To do what?'

'He claims he only has one suit at a time, and you don't seem to have a large wardrobe either.'

'I want for nothing. We eat well.'

'You can't spend even a third of what he earns.'

'I don't bother myself with business matters.'

'Most men work with a specific goal in mind. Some want a house in the country, others dream of retiring, others devote themselves to their children. He doesn't have children, does he?'

'Unfortunately, I can't have children.'

'And before you?'

'No. He's hardly known any other women. He made do with you know what. That's how I met him.'

'What does he do with his money?'

'I don't know. He must save it.'

They had in fact found a bank account in Steuvels' name, at the O. branch of the Société Générale in Rue Saint-Antoine. Almost every week, he made small deposits there, which corresponded to the sums he had been paid by his customers.

'He always worked for the pleasure of working. He's Flemish. I'm starting to understand what that means. He can spend hours on a binding just for the joy of achieving something remarkable.'

It was strange: sometimes she spoke about him in the past tense, as if the walls of the Santé had already separated him from the world, sometimes in the present, as if he was going to come home at any moment.

'Did he keep in touch with his family?'

'He never knew his father. He was brought up by an uncle, who placed him in a charitable institution when he was very young – luckily for him, because that was where he learned his trade. But they were treated harshly there, and he doesn't like talking about it.'

There was no way out from the apartment except

through the door of the workshop. To reach the court-yard, you had to go out in the street and through the arch, past the concierge's lodge.

It was amazing, back at Quai des Orfèvres, to hear Lucas juggling with all these names that Maigret could barely keep up with – Madame Salazar the concierge, Mademoi-selle Béguin the fourth-floor tenant, the cobbler, the woman who sold umbrellas, the dairy woman and her maid – all of whom he spoke about as if he had known them for ever, detailing their every habit.

'What are you cooking him for tomorrow?'

'Lamb stew. He likes eating. I think you asked me earlier what his passion is outside his work. It's probably food. And although he's sitting all day long, and doesn't take any air or exercise, I've never seen a man with such a healthy appetite.'

'Before meeting you, did he have any friends?'

'I don't think so. He never talked to me about them.'

'Did he already live here?'

'Yes. He did his own housework. Just once a week, Mad-ame Salazar came in and cleaned the place thoroughly. Maybe it's because we don't need her any more that she's never liked me.'

'Do the neighbours know?'

'What I did before? No, I mean not until Frans was arrested. It was the reporters who mentioned it.'

'Have they cold-shouldered you?'

'Some of them. But Frans was so well liked that most of them just feel sorry for us.'

That was more or less true, in a general way. If, out on

the street, they had counted up those for and those against, those for would certainly have prevailed.

But the locals didn't want it to end too soon, any more than the newspaper readers did. The greater the mystery, the fiercer the struggle between the police and Philippe Liotard, the happier people were.

'What did Alfonsi want?'

'He didn't have time to tell me. He'd only just arrived when you came in. I don't like the way he comes in here as if it's a public place, not taking his hat off, calling me by my first name. If Frans was here, he'd long since have thrown him out the door.'

'Is he jealous?'

'He doesn't like men getting too familiar.'

'Does he love you?'

'Yes, I think so.'

'Why?'

'I don't know. Maybe because I love him.'

He didn't smile. Unlike Alfonsi, he had taken his hat off. He wasn't abrupt, nor did he assume his sly air.

In that basement, he really did seem like a big man who was honestly trying to understand.

'Obviously you won't say anything that could be used against him.'

'Of course not. But I don't have anything like that to say.'

'All the same, it's obvious that a man was killed in this basement.'

'So the experts say, and I'm not educated enough to contradict them. But he wasn't killed by Frans.'

'It seems impossible it could have happened without his knowing it.'

'I know what you're going to say, but I repeat, he's innocent.'

Maigret stood up with a sigh. He was pleased that she hadn't offered him anything to drink, as most people think they have to in such circumstances.

'I'm trying to start again from scratch,' he admitted. 'My intention in coming here was to examine the premises again, inch by inch.'

'Why haven't you? Everything's been turned upside down so many times!'

'I can't face it. I may be back. I'm sure I'll have more questions to ask you.'

'You know I tell Frans everything when I visit him?'

'Yes, I understand.'

He walked up the narrow staircase, and she followed him into the workshop, which was almost dark by now. She opened the door. As she did so, they both saw Alfonsi waiting on the street corner.

'Are you going to let him in?'

'I'm wondering that myself. I'm tired.'

'Would you like me to order him to leave you alone?'

'At least for this evening.'

'Goodbye.'

She returned his goodbye, and he strode heavily over to Alfonsi. As he joined him on the corner, two young reporters were watching through the windows of the Tabac des Vosges.

'Scram!'

'Why?'

'No reason. Because she doesn't want you to disturb her again today. Understood?'

'Why are you so unpleasant to me?'

'Simply because I don't like your face.'

Maigret turned his back on him and conformed to tradition by going into the Grand Turenne and having a glass of beer.

3. The Hotel in Rue Lepic

The sun was still bright, but it was cold, the kind of dry cold that turned your breath to steam and froze your fingertips. All the same, Maigret had stood on the platform of the bus, sometimes grunting, sometimes smiling in spite of himself, as he read the morning paper.

He was early. It was barely 8.30 by his watch when he walked into the inspectors' room just as Janvier, who had been sitting on a table, was trying to get down from it and hide the newspaper he had been reading out loud.

There were five or six of them there, mainly young ones, waiting for Lucas to assign them their tasks of the day. They avoided looking at Maigret, though some stole surreptitious glances at him while finding it hard to keep a straight face.

They were not to know that he had been as amused by the article as they were, and it was to please them, because they expected it, that he assumed his grouchy air.

There was a three-column headline on the front page:

Madame Maigret's misadventure

His wife's adventure the previous day in Place d'Anvers was recounted down to the smallest detail, and all that was missing was a photograph of Madame Maigret herself, along with the little boy with whom she had been so casually entrusted.

He opened Lucas' door. Lucas too had read the article, and he had his reasons to take the matter more seriously.

'I hope you don't think it came from me? I was really surprised when I opened the paper this morning. I didn't talk to any reporter. Yesterday, after we spoke, I telephoned Lamballe in the 9th arrondissement. I told him the story, but without mentioning your wife's name, and asked him to find the taxi. By the way, he's just phoned me to say that by pure chance he's already found the driver. He's sending him to you. The man will be here in a few minutes.'

'Was there anyone in your office when you called Lamballe?'

'Probably. There's always someone. And the door to the inspectors' room was probably open. But who? It scares me to think there was a leak here.'

'I suspected as much yesterday. There was already a leak on February 21st. By the time you went to Rue de Turenne to search Steuvels' place, Philippe Liotard had been informed.'

'Who by?'

'I don't know. It must have been somebody here in the house.'

'Is that why the suitcase was gone by the time I got there?'

'More than likely.'

'In that case, why didn't they also get rid of the suit with the bloodstains?'

'Maybe they didn't think about it, or maybe they thought nobody would establish the nature of the stains. Maybe they didn't have time.'

'Would you like me to question the inspectors, chief?'

'I'll handle it.'

Lucas was still going through his mail, which was piled up on the long table he had adopted as a desk.

'Anything interesting?'

'I don't know yet. I have to check. Several tips about the suitcase, as it happens. There's an anonymous letter saying simply that it's still at the bookbinder's and we must be blind not to have found it. Then there's another that says the crux of the case is in Concarneau. And there's a five-page letter, in small handwriting, demonstrating with all kinds of arguments that the government set the whole thing up to divert attention from the cost of living.'

Maigret went into his office, took off his hat and coat and, in spite of the mild weather, shovelled coal into the only stove that remained in Quai des Orfèvres, the one he'd had so much difficulty in keeping when central heating had been installed.

Half opening the door to the inspectors' room, he called to young Lapointe, who had just arrived.

'Sit down.'

He carefully closed the door, again told Lapointe to sit down and walked three times around him, throwing him curious glances as he did so.

'Are you ambitious?'

'Yes, sir. I'd like to have a career like yours. I think they call that having great expectations, don't they?'

'Do your parents have money?'

'No. My father's a bank clerk in Meulan. He found it hard to give my sisters and me a decent upbringing.'

'Do you have a girlfriend?'

He didn't blush, didn't become flustered. 'No. Not yet. I have time. I'm only twenty-four, and I don't want to get married until I'm sure of my position.'

'Do you live alone?'

'Luckily, no. My youngest sister, Germaine, is also in Paris. She works in a publishing house on the Left Bank. We live together and in the evening she finds time to cook for both of us. That saves us money.'

'Does she have a boyfriend?'

'She's only eighteen.'

'When you went to Rue de Turenne the first time, did you come straight back here?'

He blushed suddenly, and hesitated a good long while before replying. 'No,' he admitted at last. 'I was so proud and happy to have discovered something that I caught a taxi and went via Rue du Bac to tell Germaine.'

'It's all right, son. Thank you.'

Disconcerted and anxious, Lapointe hesitated to leave. 'Why did you ask me that?'

'I ask the questions, don't I? Maybe you'll ask the questions later. Were you in Sergeant Lucas' office yesterday when he phoned the 9th arrondissement?'

'I was in the office next door, and the door was open.'

'What time did you talk to your sister?'

'How do you know that?'

'Answer the question.'

'She finishes at five. She waited for me in the Bar de la Grosse Horloge, as she often does, we had an aperitif together and then went home.'

'You didn't leave her all evening?'

'She went to the cinema with a friend.'

'Did you see this friend?'

'No. But I know her.'

'That's all. You can go.'

He would have liked to explain himself, but just then he was told that a taxi-driver was asking to see him. He was a large, ruddy-faced man in his fifties, who had probably been a coachman in his youth and who, to judge by his breath, must have had a few glasses of white wine on an empty stomach before coming.

'Inspector Lamballe told me to come and see you about the young woman.'

'How did he find out that you were the one who drove her?'

'I usually park on Place Pigalle. He spoke to all my colleagues last night, including me. I was the one who took her.'

'When and where?'

'It must have been around one o'clock. I'd just finished having lunch in a restaurant in Rue Lepic. My cab was outside. I saw a couple come out of the hotel opposite, and the woman went running straight to my taxi. She seemed disappointed when she saw it wasn't for hire. But as I was only having a liqueur, I stood up and yelled to her from across the street to wait.'

'What did her companion look like?'

'A short fat man, very well-dressed, foreign-looking. Between forty and fifty, I can't say for certain. I didn't get much of a look at him. He was turned towards her and speaking in a foreign language.'

'What language?'

'I don't know. I'm from Pantin, I've never been able to tell one lingo from another.'

'What address did she give you?'

'She was nervous and impatient. She asked me to go first to Place d'Anvers and to slow down when we got there. She kept looking out of the window.

'"Stop for a moment," she said, "and then drive on as soon as I tell you."

'She was signalling to someone. An older lady came towards us with a little boy. The young woman opened the door, let the boy in, and ordered me to drive on.'

'Did you think it was a kidnapping?'

'No. Because she spoke to the lady. Not for long. Just a few words. And the lady seemed quite relieved.'

'Where did you take the mother and the child?'

'First to Porte de Neuilly. When we got there, she changed her mind and asked me to take her to Gare Saint-Lazare.'

'Did she get out there?'

'No. She stopped me on Place Saint-Augustin. Then I got caught in a traffic jam, and I saw her in my rear-view mirror, hailing another taxi, a municipal one, but I didn't have time to get the number.'

'Why did you want to?'

'Out of habit. She was really worked up. And it isn't normal, after taking me all the way to Porte de Neuilly, to stop me on Place Saint-Augustin and then get into another cab.'

'Did she talk to the child during the ride?'

'Two or three sentences, to keep him quiet. Is there a reward?'

'Maybe. I don't know yet.'

'It's just that I've lost a morning.'

Maigret handed over a banknote. A few minutes later, he walked into the office of the director of the Police Judiciaire, where the daily report had started. The heads of the various departments were there, sitting around the large mahogany desk, talking calmly about their current cases.

'What about you, Maigret? This Steuvels of yours?'

From their smiles, it was clear they'd all read that morning's article, and again, to please them, he put on a grouchy air.

It was 9.30. The telephone rang. The director answered, then held out the receiver to Maigret.

'Torrence, for you.'

Torrence's voice at the other end of the line sounded excited. 'Is that you, chief? Have you found the woman in the white hat yet? The paper just arrived from Paris and I read the article. The description corresponds to someone who was here.'

'Go on!'

'As there was no way of getting anything out of that stupid postmistress, who claims she doesn't have a good memory, I started looking in the hotels and rooming houses and questioning garage mechanics and railway staff.'

'I know.'

'It isn't the season yet, and most people who come to Concarneau either live in the region or are the kinds of people you'd expect, travelling salesman or—'

'Keep it short.'

Around him, all conversation had ceased.

'I told myself that if anyone had come from Paris, or wherever, to send the telegram—'

'Please, I've already understood.'

'Well, a young woman in a blue tailored suit and a white hat arrived here the very same evening the telegram was sent. She got off the train at four o'clock, and the telegram was handed in at a quarter to five.'

'Did she have any luggage with her?'

'No. Wait. She didn't check into a hotel. Do you know the Hôtel du Chien Jaune, at the end of the quay? She had dinner there, and then sat in a corner of the coffee shop until eleven. She got back on the train at 11.40.'

'Did you check?'

'I haven't had time yet but I'm pretty sure, because she left the coffee shop just in time and she'd asked for the railway timetable immediately after dinner.'

'Did she speak to anyone?'

'Just the waitress. She was reading all the time, even while she was eating.'

'Were you able to find out what kind of book she was reading?'

'No. The waitress says she had an accent, but doesn't know which one. What shall I do?'

'See the postmistress again, obviously.'

'And then?'

'Phone me or phone Lucas if I'm not in the office, then come back here.'

'OK, chief. Do you also think it's her?'

As he hung up, there was a little gleam of joviality in Maigret's eyes. 'Madame Maigret may have given us a lead,' he said. 'Would you mind, chief? I have some things to check urgently.'

By chance, Lapointe was still in the inspectors' office, looking distinctly worried.

'Come with me!'

They took one of the taxis parked outside. Young Lapointe was still nervous: this was the first time Maigret had ever taken him with him like this.

'The corner of Place Blanche and Rue Lepic.'

It was the time of day when, in Montmartre, and Rue Lepic in particular, the kerbs were packed with market stalls piled high with fruit and vegetables, all smelling nicely of the land and of spring.

On the left, Maigret recognized the little fixed-price restaurant where the taxi-driver had had lunch and, opposite, the Hôtel Beauséjour, the only part of it visible being a narrow door between two shops, a pork butcher's and a grocer's.

Rooms by the month, week and day.
Running water. Central heating. Reasonable prices.

There was a glass door at the end of the corridor, then a staircase with a sign on the wall saying Office and a hand painted in black pointing to the top of the stairs.

The office was on the mezzanine, a narrow room looking out on the street, with keys hanging from a board.

'Is there anyone here?' he called.

The smell reminded him of the time when, round about the same age as Lapointe was now, he had worked in the hotels squad and spent his days going from rooming house to rooming house. They always smelled of laundry and sweat, unmade beds, pails of dirty water, and food cooked over a spirit lamp.

A dishevelled-looking red-haired woman leaned over the banister. 'What is it?' Then, immediately, realizing it was the police, she announced sullenly, 'I'm coming!'

For a while longer, she walked about upstairs, moving buckets and brushes. At last she appeared, buttoning up her blouse over her protuberant breasts. From up close, it was clear that her hair was almost white at the roots.

'What is it? They checked me yesterday. I only have quiet people here. You're from the hotels squad, are you?'

He didn't answer that question, but described, in as much detail as the driver's testimony allowed, the companion of the woman in the white hat.

'Do you know him?'

'Maybe. I'm not sure. What's his name?'

'That's what I'm trying to find out.'

'Do you want to see my register?'

'I want you to tell me first of all if you have a guest who looks like him.'

'The only one I can think of is Monsieur Levine.'

'Who's he?'

'I don't know. Someone decent, anyway. He paid a week in advance.'

'Is he still here?'

'No. He left yesterday.'

'Alone?'

'With the boy, of course.'

'And the woman?'

'You mean the nurse?'

'Hold on. Why don't we start from the beginning, we'll save time that way.'

'That's fine by me, I don't have time to spare. What has Monsieur Levine done?'

'Would you just answer my questions, please? When did he arrive?'

'Four days ago. You can check in the register. I told him I didn't have any rooms and it was true. He insisted. I asked him how long it was for and he told me he'd pay a week in advance.'

'How were you able to put him up, if you didn't have any rooms?'

Maigret knew the answer, but he wanted to make her say it. In that kind of establishment, they usually kept the rooms on the first floor for passing trade: couples who only needed them for an hour or less.

'There are always the "casual" rooms,' she replied, using the established term.

'Was the boy with him?'

'Not at that time. He went to fetch him and came back

with him an hour later. I asked him how he was going to manage with such a young child and he told me that a nurse he knew would look after him for most of the day.'

'Did he show you his passport and his identity card?'

According to regulations, she should have asked for these documents, but she obviously didn't do things by the book.

'He filled out his form himself. I could see straight away he was a respectable man. You're not going to give me any trouble, are you?'

'Not necessarily. How was the nurse dressed?'

'In a blue tailored suit.'

'With a white hat?'

'Yes. She'd come in the morning to give the boy his bath then go out with him.'

'What about Monsieur Levine?'

'He'd stay in his room until eleven or twelve. I think he'd go back to bed. Then he'd go out and I wouldn't see him again during the day.'

'What about the boy?'

'I wouldn't see him either. Not until about seven in the evening. She was the one who brought him back and put him to bed. She'd lie down fully dressed on the bed and wait for Monsieur Levine to get back.'

'What time did he usually get back?'

'Not until one in the morning.'

'And then she'd leave?'

'Yes.'

'Do you know where she lived?'

'No. All I know, because I saw it, is that she took a taxi when she left.'

'Was she intimate with your tenant?'

'You mean did they sleep together? I'm not sure. I got the impression they might have done. They're entitled, aren't they?'

'What nationality did Monsieur Levine put on his card?'

'French. He told me he'd been in France for a long time and was naturalized.'

'Where was he from?'

'I can't remember. Your colleague from the hotels squad took the forms away yesterday, like every Tuesday. From Bordeaux, if I'm not mistaken.'

'What happened yesterday at midday?'

'At midday, I don't know.'

'And in the morning?'

'Someone came to ask for him about ten o'clock. The woman and the boy had been gone for a while.'

'Who was the person who came?'

'I didn't ask his name. He wasn't well dressed, looked a bit seedy to me.'

'French?'

'Definitely. I told him the number of the room.'

'Had he ever been before?'

'Nobody had ever been, except the nurse.'

'Did he have a southern accent?'

'More of a Parisian accent. You know, one of those people who stop you on the boulevards to sell you dirty postcards or take you God knows where.'

'Did he stay for a long time?'

'He stayed on his own and Monsieur Levine left.'

'With his luggage?'

'How do you know that? I was surprised to see him take his luggage with him.'

'Did he have a lot?'

'Four suitcases.'

'Brown?'

'Almost all suitcases are brown, aren't they? They were good quality, though. At least two of them were genuine leather.'

'What did he tell you?'

'That he had to leave in a hurry, that he was leaving Paris the same day, but that he'd be back in a while to take the boy's things.'

'How soon after that did he come back?'

'About an hour. The woman was with him.'

'Didn't it surprise you not to see the boy?'

'You know that too?'

She was becoming cagier, starting to suspect that this was something important, and that the police knew more than Maigret was prepared to tell her.

'The three of them stayed in the room for a while, talking quite loudly.'

'As if they were arguing?'

'As if they were discussing something, anyway.'

'In French?'

'No.'

'Did the Parisian take part in the conversation?'

'Not much. In fact, he came out first, and I didn't see him again. Then Monsieur Levine and the woman left. As

I was in their way, he thanked me and told me he was planning to come back in a few days.'

'Didn't that strike you as strange?'

'If you'd been running a hotel like this one for eighteen years, nothing would ever strike you as strange.'

'Was it you who tidied their room after they left?'

'I went there with the maid.'

'Did you find anything?'

'Cigarette ends everywhere. He smoked more than fifty a day. American ones. And newspapers. He bought almost all the papers that come out in Paris.'

'No foreign papers?'

'No. I thought of that.'

'So you were intrigued?'

'It's always nice to know.'

'What else did you find?'

'Rubbish, as usual, a broken comb, torn underwear . . .'

'Initialled?'

'No. It was a child's.'

'Good underwear?'

'Quite good, yes. Better than I usually see here.'

'I'll be back to talk to you.'

'Why?'

'Because I'm sure there are things you've forgotten that'll come back to you when you think about it. You've always been on good terms with the police, have you? Never had any bother from the hotels squad?'

'I get the picture. But I don't know anything else.'

'Goodbye for now.'

He and Lapointe found themselves back outside on the

sunlit pavement, surrounded by the commotion of the market.

'How about an aperitif?' Maigret suggested.

'I don't drink.'

'Good for you. Have you thought things over since before?'

Lapointe realized Maigret wasn't talking about what they had just found out at the hotel. 'Yes.'

'And?'

'I'll talk to her this evening.'

'Do you know who it was?'

'I have a friend who's a reporter on the very same paper that carried that item. But I didn't see him yesterday. And I never talk to him about what happens at the Quai. He likes to tease me about that.'

'Does your sister know him?'

'Yes. I didn't think they were going out together. If I tell my father, he'll make her go back to Meulan.'

'What's the reporter's name?'

'Bizard, Antoine Bizard. He's alone in Paris too. His family live in Corrèze. He's two years younger than me, and already has his name on some of the things he writes.'

'Do you see your sister at lunchtime?'

'It depends. When I'm free and I'm not too far from Rue du Bac, I have lunch with her in a dairy near her office.'

'Go there today. Tell her what we found out this morning.'

'Do I have to?'

'Yes.'

'What if she passes it on again?'

'She will.'

'Is that what you want?'

'Go. And be nice to her. Don't act as if you suspect her.'

'But I can't let her go out with a young man. My father made it quite clear that—'

'Go.'

For the pleasure of it, Maigret walked down Rue Notre-Dame-de-Lorette and only took the taxi when he reached Faubourg Montmartre, having first dropped into a brasserie for a beer.

'Quai des Orfèvres.'

Then he changed his mind and knocked on the glass.

'Go via Rue de Turenne.'

He saw Steuvels' shop. The door was closed: Fernande must, as every morning, be on her way to the Santé, with her stacked pans.

'Stop for a moment.'

Janvier was at the bar of the Grand Turenne, and winked when he saw him. What had Lucas asked him to check this time? He was deep in conversation with the cobbler and two plasterers in white overalls. From a distance, you could recognize the milky colour of Pernods.

'Turn left. Go via Place des Vosges and Rue de Birague.'

That took him past the Tabac des Vosges, where Alfonsi was sitting alone at a table near the window.

'Are you getting out?'

'Yes, but I'd like you to wait.'

In the end, he went into the Grand Turenne to have a word with Janvier.

'Alfonsi's opposite. Have you seen any reporters this morning?'

'Two or three.'

'Do you know them?'

'Not all of them.'

'Will you be busy for long?'

'It's nothing important. And if you have anything else you want me to do, I'm free. I wanted to talk to the cobbler.'

They had moved sufficiently far from the group and were talking in low voices.

'An idea occurred to me earlier after reading that item. Obviously, the man talks a lot. He's determined to be an important person, and he'd make things up if he had to. Not to mention that every time he says something, he gets a few drinks out of it. As he lives just opposite the book-binder's and also works by the window, I asked him if Steuvels ever had any women visitors.'

'What did he say?'

'Not many. The one he particularly remembers is an old lady. She must be rich because she comes in a limousine with a liveried chauffeur who leaves her books there. But then, about a month ago, there was a very elegant woman in a fur coat. I made sure to ask if she'd only come the once. He says no, she came back about two weeks ago, in a blue tailored suit and a white hat. It was a day when the weather was very good and there was apparently an article in the newspaper about the chestnut tree on Boulevard Saint-Germain.'

'We can find it.'

'That's what I thought.'

'Did she go down into the basement?'

'No. But I'm a bit suspicious. It's obvious he also read this morning's article, and it's quite possible he's making this up to draw attention to himself. What would you like me to do?'

'Keep your eye on Alfonsi. Stay with him all day. Make a list of the people he talks to.'

'And he mustn't know that I'm following him?'

'It doesn't matter if he knows.'

'What if he talks to me?'

'Answer him.'

Maigret left with the smell of Pernod in his nostrils and his taxi dropped him at the Quai, where he found Lucas having sandwiches for lunch. There were two glasses of beer on the desk and Maigret shamelessly took one.

'Torrence has just phoned. The postmistress thinks she remembers a female customer in a white hat, but can't say for sure she was the one who handed in the telegram. According to Torrence, even if she was sure, she wouldn't say.'

'Is he on his way back?'

'He'll be in Paris tonight.'

'Would you mind calling the municipal taxi office? There's another taxi to find, maybe two.'

Had Madame Maigret, who had another appointment with the dentist, left early, like the other days, to spend a few minutes on the bench in Square d'Anvers?

Maigret didn't go home for lunch. Tempted by Lucas'
sandwiches, he had some sent up to him from the Brasserie Dauphine.

That was usually a good sign.

4. Fernande's Adventure

Red-eyed and haggard, like someone who'd slept on a bench in a third-class waiting room, young Lapointe had such a look of distress on his face when Maigret walked into the inspectors' office that he immediately drew the boy into his.

'The whole Hôtel Beauséjour story is in the paper,' Lapointe said glumly.

'So much the better! I would have been disappointed if it wasn't.'

So it had been deliberate on Maigret's part, talking to him as if he were a veteran, someone like Lucas or Torrence, for instance.

'These are people we know almost nothing about, not even if they really were involved in the case. There's a woman, a little boy, a rather large man, and another who's rather seedy-looking. Are they still in Paris? We have no idea. If they are, they've probably split up. If the woman takes off her white hat and separates from the boy, we'll never recognize her. Are you following me?'

'Yes, sir. I think I understand. All the same, I find it hard to believe that my sister went and saw that young man again last night.'

'You can deal with your sister later. Right now, you're working with me. This morning's article is going to scare them. One of two things will happen: either they'll stay in their hole, if they have one, or they'll look for a safer hideout. Whatever the case, our one chance is for them to do something to give themselves away.'

'Yes.'

At that moment, Judge Dossin phoned to express his surprise at the newspaper's revelations, and Maigret had to explain his reasoning all over again.

'Everyone's been alerted, your honour, the stations, the airports, the hotels squad, the traffic police. Upstairs in Records, Moers is looking for photographs that might correspond to these people. We're questioning the taxi-drivers and, in case our characters have a car, the garage owners.'

'You really think there's a connection with the Steuvels case?'

'It's a lead. We've had so many that have got us nowhere.'

'I've summoned Steuvels for eleven o'clock this morning. His lawyer will be there as usual. He won't let me say two words to his client without his being there.'

'Is it OK if I come up for a moment while you're questioning him?'

'Liotard will object, but come up anyway. As long as it doesn't look premeditated.'

The strange thing was that Maigret hadn't yet met this Liotard, even though he'd become something like his personal enemy, in the press anyway.

Once again this morning, all the newspapers had published the young lawyer's comments on the latest developments in the case.

Maigret is a policeman of the old school, from a time when those gentlemen in the Quai des Orfèvres could happily beat a man up until he was so exhausted he confessed, keep him in custody for weeks on end, and delve shamelessly into people's private lives, a time when all kinds of tricks were considered fair.

He is the only one who has not realized that these days such tricks are all too familiar to an informed public.

What does this whole case boil down to?

He has let himself be led astray by an anonymous letter, the work of a practical joker. He has had an honest man locked up but still has not managed to bring any serious charges against him.

He is stubborn. Rather than admit defeat, he is trying to gain time, to please the gallery, even bringing Madame Maigret into it and presenting the public with episodes from a cheap novel.

Believe me, gentlemen, Maigret is a man who has outlived his time!

'Stay with me, son,' Maigret said to young Lapointe. 'Just make sure that before you leave this evening, you ask me what you can tell your sister, all right?'

'I'll never tell her anything again.'

'You'll tell her what I ask you to tell her.'

Lapointe was now serving as his adjutant. This was all too appropriate, as the Police Judiciaire was becoming ever more like a military headquarters.

Lucas' office, the Grand Turenne, remained the command post, with couriers arriving from all the other departments. Downstairs, several officers from the hotels squad were going through their records in search of a Levine or anything connected with the trio and the child.

The previous night, in most rooming houses the guests had had the unpleasant surprise of being woken by the police and having their documents examined. The operation had ended with some fifty men and women whose papers weren't in order finishing the night in the cells at headquarters, where they were now waiting in line to be measured and photographed.

In the railway stations, travellers were being given the once-over without their realizing it, and two hours after the newspapers had appeared the telephone calls began, soon coming in so thick and fast that Lucas had to assign an inspector to help him.

People had seen the boy everywhere, in the most diverse corners of Paris and the suburbs, some in the company of the woman in the white hat, others with the man with the foreign accent.

Passers-by would suddenly rush up to a policeman.

'Come quickly! The boy's on the corner of the street.'

Everything was checked, everything had to be checked if they didn't want to miss their chance. Three inspectors had set off early to question the garage owners.

And all night, men from the vice squad had been joining in. Hadn't the manageress of the Beauséjour said that her guest didn't usually get back before one in the morning?

In order to find out if he was a regular in nightclubs, they had questioned the barmen and the hostesses.

And now Maigret, after the daily report in the chief's

office, was coming and going throughout the building, almost always accompanied by Lapointe: downstairs to the hotels squad, upstairs to see Moers in Records, listening to a phone call here, a statement there.

It was just after ten o'clock when a driver from the municipal taxi office phoned. He hadn't called earlier because he'd been out of town, all the way to Dreux, driving a sick old lady who didn't want to take the train.

It was he who had picked up the young woman and the little boy in Place Saint-Augustin. He remembered them well.

'Where did you drive them?'

'To the corner of Rue Montmartre and the Grands Boulevards.'

'Was someone waiting for them there?'

'I didn't see anyone.'

'Do you know which way they went?'

'I lost sight of them in the crowd.'

There were several hotels in the vicinity.

'Call the hotels squad again!' Maigret said to Lapointe. 'They need to take a thorough look at the area around the Carrefour Montmartre. You understand now, don't you? If they don't panic, if they don't move, we have no chance of finding them.'

Torrence was back from Concarneau, but had gone straight to Rue de Turenne, to get back into the atmosphere, as he put it.

As for Janvier, he had sent in his report and was still tailing Alfonsi.

The previous evening, Alfonsi had met up with Philippe

Liotard in a restaurant in Rue Richelieu, where they'd had a good dinner and a quiet chat. They had later been joined by two women, neither of them looking anything like the young woman in the white hat. One was Liotard's secretary, a tall blonde who looked like a starlet. The other had left with Alfonsi.

They had gone together to the cinema, near the Opéra, then to a cabaret in Rue Blanche where they had stayed until two in the morning.

After which Alfonsi had taken his companion to the hotel in Rue de Douai where he lived.

Janvier had taken a room in the same hotel. He had just phoned.

'They aren't up yet. I'm still waiting.'

Just before eleven, Lapointe was to discover, as he followed Maigret, some parts of the Quai des Orfèvres he didn't know. They had been walking along a deserted corridor on the ground floor, whose windows looked out on the courtyard, when Maigret stopped at a corner and motioned to him to be quiet.

A Black Maria was just entering the courtyard, passing under the arch of the section where the cells were. Three or four gendarmes were waiting, smoking their cigarettes. Two others got out of the Black Maria. The first person they brought out was a big brute of a fellow with a low forehead, handcuffs on his wrists. Maigret didn't know him, had never had dealings with him.

Then came a frail-looking old woman who could have been a chair attendant in a church, but whom he had arrested at least twenty times as a pickpocket. She followed her gendarme like a regular, scampering along in her over-large skirts, heading straight for the area where the examining magistrates had their offices.

The sun was bright, the air blue in the patches of shadow. There was an occasional breath of spring, and a few flies were already buzzing about.

They saw Frans Steuvels' red hair. He wasn't wearing any hat or cap, and his suit was somewhat rumpled. He stopped, as if surprised by the sunlight, and you could see his half-closed eyes behind his big glasses. He was hand-cuffed, just like the brute: the regulation had been strictly observed ever since some prisoners had escaped from that same courtyard, the last one through the corridors of the Palais de Justice itself.

With his round back and slack figure, Steuvels was the very image of those intellectual artisans who read every-thing they can get their hands on and have no other passion besides their work.

One of the guards handed him a lighted cigarette and he thanked him and took a few satisfied puffs, filling his lungs with air and tobacco smoke.

He must have been behaving himself, because they were gentle with him, giving him time to relax before leading him towards the building. For his part, he didn't seem to bear any grudge towards his guards, displayed no resent-ment, no emotion.

There was a small basis of truth in the interview Maître Liotard had given. At other times, Maigret would have pursued his investigation to the end before handing the man over to the examining magistrate.

In fact, if Liotard hadn't come running after the first interrogation, Maigret would have seen Steuvels again several times, and would have had the opportunity to study him.

He barely knew him, having been alone with him for a mere ten or twelve hours, at a time when he didn't yet know anything about him or the case.

Rarely had he been confronted with a suspect so calm, so self-possessed, and who was clearly not putting it on.

Steuvels had waited for the questions, head bowed, with the air of wanting to understand, and he had looked at Maigret as he might have looked at a lecturer presenting complicated ideas.

Then he had taken the time to think and when he had spoken, it was in a soft, slightly muffled voice, in sentences that were meticulous but unaffected.

He hadn't lost patience, like most people Maigret interrogated, and, when the same question came back for the twentieth time, he had replied in the same terms, with remarkable tranquillity.

Maigret would have liked to get to know him better, but for the past three weeks the man hadn't belonged to him any more; he had belonged to Judge Dossin, who would summon him, along with his lawyer, twice a week on average.

Deep down, Steuvels must have been a shy man. The oddest part of it was that Judge Dossin was a shy man, too. Seeing the initial G. in front of his name, Maigret had ventured one day to ask him his first name, and the tall, distinguished magistrate had blushed.

'Don't repeat this, because they'd start calling me "the angel", just as my classmates did at school, and then my fellow students at law school. My first name is Gabriel.'

'Right,' Maigret said now to Lapointe. 'You're going to wait for me in my office and take any call that comes in.'

He didn't go straight upstairs, but roamed the corridors for a while with his pipe between his teeth and his hands in his pockets, like a man who feels at home, shaking a hand here, a hand there.

When he judged that the interrogation must already be in progress, he went to the magistrates' section and knocked at Judge Dossin's door.

'May I?'

'Come in, Detective Chief Inspector Maigret.'

A man had stood up. He was short and thin, very thin, with an overly studied elegance, and Maigret recognized him immediately from having seen photographs of him in the newspapers. He was young, but assumed a self-important air to look older, affecting a confidence that didn't fit his age.

He was quite good-looking, with dark skin, black hair and long nostrils that sometimes quivered, and he looked people in the eyes as if determined to make them lower their gaze.

'Monsieur Maigret, I presume?'

'That's correct, Maître Liotard.'

'If it's me you're looking for, I'll be pleased to speak to you after the interrogation.'

Frans Steuvels had remained seated opposite the judge,

70

waiting. He had merely glanced at Maigret, then at the clerk who sat at the end of the desk with his pen in his hand.

'I'm not looking for you in particular. As it happens, I'm looking for a chair.'

He took one by the back and sat down astride it, still smoking his pipe.

'Do you intend to stay here?'

'Unless the examining magistrate asks me to leave.'

'Stay, Maigret.'

'I protest. If the interrogation is to continue in these conditions, then I must express my reservations. The presence of a police officer in this office is evidently meant to intimidate my client.'

Maigret refrained from murmuring, 'Just keep singing!' but gave the young lawyer an ironic look. Liotard clearly didn't believe a word he was saying. It was all part of his strategy. At every interrogation so far, he had raised points of law, for the most trivial or extravagant of reasons.

'There's no rule against an officer from the Police Judiciaire being present at an interrogation. So if you don't mind, we'll resume where we left off.'

All the same, Judge Dossin was influenced by Maigret's presence and took a while to find his place in his own notes.

'I was asking you, Monsieur Steuvels, if you're in the habit of buying your clothes ready-made or if you have a tailor.'

Steuvels thought for a moment, then replied, 'It depends.'

'On what?'

'I don't really think much about clothes. When I need a suit, I sometimes buy it ready-made, just as I've sometimes had it made for me.'

'By what tailor?'

'I had a suit several years ago that was made by a neighbour, a Polish Jew. I haven't seen him for a while. I think he went to America.'

'Was it a blue suit?'

'No, it was grey.'

'How long did you wear it?'

'Two or three years, I can't remember.'

'What about your blue suit?'

'It must be ten years since I last bought a blue suit.'

'But some of your neighbours saw you in blue not so long ago.'

'They must have confused my suit and my overcoat.'

It was true that a navy-blue overcoat had been found in the apartment.

'When did you buy that overcoat?'

'Last winter.'

'Wasn't it odd to buy a blue overcoat when you only had a brown suit? The two colours aren't particularly well matched.'

'I don't pay that much attention to my appearance.'

During this time, Maître Liotard had been looking defiantly at Maigret, staring at him so fixedly it was as if he wanted to hypnotize him. Then, as he would have done in court to impress the jury, he gave a sarcastic smile and shrugged his shoulders.

'Why won't you admit that the suit found in the wardrobe belongs to you?'

'Because it doesn't belong to me.'

'Then how do you explain why it was there, when to all intents and purposes you never leave home, and your bedroom can only be reached through the workshop?'

'I can't explain it.'

'Let's be reasonable, Monsieur Steuvels. I'm not trying to trap you. This is at least the third time we've tackled this subject. If you are to be believed, someone got into your home without your knowledge and left two human teeth in the ashes in your stove. What's more, this person chose the day when your wife was away and, for her to be away, he'd had to go to Concarneau – or dispatch an associate – to send a telegram saying that her mother was ill. Wait, that's not all.

'Not only were you alone at home, which practically never happens, but you made such a big fire in the stove, that day and the following day, that it took you five trips to carry all the ashes to the dustbins.

'Regarding that, we have a statement by your concierge, Madame Salazar, who has no reason to lie, and who can see all her tenants' comings and goings quite easily from her lodge. On Sunday morning, you took five trips, each time with a large bucket full of ashes.

'She thought you'd been doing the spring cleaning and were burning old papers.

'We have another statement, from Mademoiselle Béguin who lives on the top floor, and who claims that your chimney was smoking the whole of Sunday. Black smoke, she insisted. She opened her window at a certain point and noticed an unpleasant smell.'

'Isn't this Mademoiselle Béguin, who is sixty-eight years old, known locally for being simple-minded?' Liotard asked, extinguishing his cigarette in the ashtray and choosing another from a silver case. 'Allow me also to observe that for four days, as the weather reports from 15th, 16th, 17th and 18th February clearly show, the temperature in Paris and the surrounding region was abnormally low.'

'That doesn't explain the teeth. Nor does it explain the presence of a blue suit in the wardrobe, or the bloodstains on that suit.'

'You're making these accusations and it's for you to prove them. But you can't even prove that suit really belongs to my client.'

'Would you allow me to ask a question, your honour?'

Dossin turned to Liotard, who didn't have time to object, because Maigret had already turned to Steuvels and was asking:

'When did you first hear of Maître Philippe Liotard?'

Liotard stood up to counter-attack, but Maigret went on impassively:

'When I finished questioning you on the evening of your arrest, or rather in the early hours of the morning, and I asked you if you wanted a lawyer, you replied in the affirmative and designated Maître Liotard.'

'A prisoner has a perfect right to choose the lawyer he wishes, and if that question is asked again, I'll be obliged to refer the matter to the Bar Council.'

'Refer away! It's you I'm asking, Steuvels. You haven't answered.

'It wouldn't have been surprising if you'd mentioned the name of some famous lawyer, but you didn't.

'You didn't look through any directory while you were in my office, and you didn't ask anybody.

'Maître Liotard doesn't live in your neighbourhood. I don't think his name had ever appeared in the newspapers up until three weeks ago.'

'I object!'

'Please do. But tell me, Steuvels, had you ever heard of Maître Liotard on the morning of the 21st, before my inspector came to see you? If yes, tell me when and where.'

'Don't answer that.'

Steuvels hesitated, round-shouldered, observing Maigret through his big glasses.

'You refuse to answer? All right. I'll ask you another question. Did anyone phone you on the afternoon of the 21st and tell you about Maître Liotard?'

Steuvels was still hesitating.

'Or, if you prefer, did you telephone anyone? Let me take you back into the atmosphere of that day, which had begun like any other day. It was sunny and very mild, so you didn't light your stove. You were at work by the window when my inspector appeared and asked if he could visit the premises, using some pretext or other.'

'You admit it!' Liotard cut in.

'Yes, maître, I admit it. But I'm not asking you the questions.

'You immediately realized that the police were interested in you, Steuvels.

'At that time, there was a brown suitcase in your workshop, but it had gone by the time Sergeant Lucas came back in the evening with a search warrant.

'Who phoned you? Who alerted you? Who came to see you between Inspector Lapointe and Sergeant Lucas?

'I've checked the list of people you're in the habit of phoning, whose numbers you had written down in a notebook. I've checked your registers. The name Liotard doesn't appear among your customers either.

'But he came to see you that very day. Did you call him or did someone you know send him?'

'I forbid you to reply.'

But Steuvels gestured impatiently. 'He came of his own accord.'

'This is Maître Liotard you're talking about, isn't it?'

Steuvels looked around, and there was a gleam in his eye, as if he were taking a personal delight in embarrassing his lawyer. 'Maître Liotard, yes.'

Liotard turned to the clerk, who was still writing. 'You have no right to record these answers. They have nothing to do with the case. Yes, it's true, I went to see Steuvels, whose reputation I was familiar with, to ask him if he could do some bookbinding for me. Isn't that correct?'

'Yes, it is.'

Why on earth was there a wicked little flame in Steuvels' clear eyes?

'It was about an ex-libris with the family coat of arms.

That's right, Monsieur Maigret, my grandfather was the Comte de Liotard. He renounced his title voluntarily when he was ruined. Anyway, I wanted a family coat of arms, and I went to see Steuvels, because I knew he was the best bookbinder in Paris, even though I'd been told he was very busy.'

'Did you talk to him about this coat of arms?'

'Forgive me, but you now seem to be questioning me. We're in your office, Monsieur Dossin, and I don't intend to be taken to task by a policeman. I already expressed my reservations when he started questioning my client. But that a member of the bar should—'

'Do you have any other questions to ask Monsieur Steuvels, Inspector Maigret?'

'No questions. I'm grateful to you.'

The funny thing was that Maigret still had the impression Steuvels wasn't angry about what had happened and was even looking at him with a new-found liking.

As for Liotard, he sat down, seized a file and pretended to become engrossed in it.

'You can come and see me whenever you like, Maître Liotard. Do you know my office? The last one on the left, at the end of the corridor.'

He smiled at Judge Dossin, who didn't look very comfortable, and headed for the little door leading from the Palais de Justice to the Police Judiciaire.

The place was more like a beehive than ever, with telephones ringing behind doors, people waiting in every corner, inspectors hurrying along the corridors.

'I think someone's waiting for you in your office, sir.'

When he opened the door, he found Fernande in conversation with young Lapointe, who was sitting in Maigret's seat, listening to her and taking notes. Embarrassed, he stood up. Fernande was plainly dressed, in a belted beige gabardine coat and a hat of the same material.

'How is he?' she asked. 'Have you just seen him? Is he still upstairs?'

'He's very well. He admits that Liotard came to the workshop on the afternoon of the 21st.'

'Something much worse than that has just happened,' she said. 'Please take what I'm going to tell you seriously. This morning, I left Rue de Turenne as usual to take him his dinner at the Santé. You know the little enamelled pans I put them in.

'I caught the Métro at Saint-Paul and changed at Châtelet. I'd bought a newspaper on the way, but hadn't had time to read it yet.

'There was a seat free next to the door. I sat down and started reading, I'm sure you know which article.

'I'd put the stacked pans on the floor next to me, and I could feel the heat against my leg.

'A few stations before the Gare Montparnasse, a lot of people got on, most of them with suitcases. They must all have been going to catch a train.

'I was so engrossed in my reading, I wasn't paying attention to what was happening around me when I had the impression somebody was touching the pans.

'I just had time to notice a hand trying to put back the metal handle.

'I stood up and turned to the person next to me. We

were just coming into Montparnasse, where I had to change. Almost everybody was getting out.

'I don't know how he did it, but he managed to overturn the pans and slip away on to the platform before I could see his face.

'The food spilled all over. I've brought you the pans. Apart from the one underneath, they're more or less empty.

'Look for yourself. There's a metal strip with a handle which keeps them together.

'It didn't open by itself.

'I'm sure someone was following me and tried to poison the food meant for Frans.'

'Take it to the lab,' Maigret said to Lapointe.

'They might not find anything. They must have tried to put the poison in the top pan, and that's empty. But you do believe me, don't you, inspector? You know I've always been honest with you.'

'Always?'

'As honest as possible. This time it's Frans' life that's at stake. Those bastards want to get him out of the way, and they tried to use me without my knowing.'

She sounded extremely bitter.

'If only I hadn't been engrossed in my newspaper, I might have seen the man. All that I know is that he was wearing a coat about the same colour as mine and worn-out black shoes.'

'Young?'

'Not very young. Not old either. Middle-aged. Or ageless, if you know what I mean. There was a stain near the shoulder of his coat, I noticed it as he was getting away.'

'Tall? Thin?'

'Fairly short. Average height at most. He looked like a rat, that's what I really thought.'

'And you're sure you've never seen him before?'

She thought this over. 'No. I can't recall him from anywhere.' Then she seemed to have second thoughts. 'It's just come back to me. I was reading the item about the woman with the little boy and the Hôtel Beauséjour. He made me think of one of the two men, the one the hotel owner said looked like a seller of dirty postcards. You're not laughing at me?'

'No.'

'You don't think I'm making this up?'

'No.'

'Do you think they tried to kill him?'

'It's possible.'

'What are you going to do?'

'I don't know yet.'

Lapointe came back and announced that the lab wouldn't have their report ready for several hours.

'Do you think it's best if he makes do with the food in the prison?'

'That might be wise.'

'He's going to wonder why I haven't sent him his meal. I won't see him for another two days, when I visit him.'

She wasn't crying, wasn't putting on airs, but her dark eyes had rings under them and were filled with anxiety and distress.

'Come with me.'

He winked at Lapointe, then led her upstairs and along corridors that grew increasingly deserted as they advanced. With difficulty, he opened a little window looking out on the courtyard, where a Black Maria was waiting.

'He'll be down soon. Will you excuse me? I have things to do upstairs . . .'

With a gesture, he pointed to the upper floors.

Incredulous, she watched him walk away, then gripped the bars with both hands, trying to see as far as possible in the direction from where Steuvels was going to emerge.

5. *Something to do with a Hat*

It was refreshing to leave the offices, with their doors slamming ceaselessly as the inspectors went in and out and all the telephones in use at the same time, and climb the always deserted staircase towards the upper floors of the Palais de Justice, where the labs and the records department were located.

It was already getting dark, and on the dimly lit stairs, which resembled some secret staircase in a castle, Maigret was preceded by his own gigantic shadow.

In a corner of an attic room, Moers, a visor over his forehead, his big glasses in front of his eyes, was working beneath a lamp which he would move closer to him or push back by tugging on a wire.

Moers hadn't been to Rue de Turenne to question the neighbours, hadn't drunk Pernod or white wine in any of the three bars, had never tailed anybody in the street or spent the night standing in front of a closed door.

He never got upset or excited, but it was quite possible he would still be bent over his desk tomorrow morning. He had once spent three whole days and nights there.

Without a word, Maigret grabbed a straw-bottomed chair, came and sat down next to Moers, lit his pipe and puffed on it gently. Hearing a regular noise on a fanlight above his head, he realized that the weather had changed and it had started to rain.

'Look at these, chief,' Moers said, holding out a bundle of photographs as if they were a pack of cards.

He had done a magnificent job, alone here in his corner. With the vague descriptions he had been given, he had somehow brought to life and even given personalities to three people of whom almost nothing was known: the fat, dark-skinned, well-dressed foreigner, the young woman in the white hat, and the accomplice who looked like 'a seller of dirty postcards'.

To do so, he had hundreds of thousands of records at his disposal, but he was probably the only person to remember them well enough to achieve what he had just so patiently achieved.

The first packet, which Maigret examined, comprised some forty photographs of fat, well-groomed men of the Greek or Middle Eastern type, with smooth skin and rings on their fingers.

'I'm not too happy with those,' Moers sighed, as if he had been given the task of casting a film. 'You can try them all the same. But I prefer these.'

There were only about fifteen photographs in the second packet, and they were cause for congratulations, so closely did they resemble the person described by the owner of the Hôtel Beauséjour.

Looking at the backs, Maigret learned the professions of these characters. Two or three were racing tipsters. There was a pickpocket he knew personally, having once arrested him on a bus, and an individual who solicited at the doors of big hotels for certain specialized establishments.

There was a self-satisfied little gleam in Moers' eyes. 'Amusing, isn't it? For the woman, I have almost nothing, because our photographs don't include hats. But I'll keep going.'

Maigret slipped the photographs into his pocket and lingered a moment longer, for the sheer pleasure of it, then sighed and walked into the lab next door, where they were still working on the food in Fernande's pans.

They hadn't discovered anything. Either the story had been completely made up, for what purpose he couldn't guess, or they hadn't had time to put the poison in, or else the poison had fallen into the part that had completely overturned in the Métro carriage.

Maigret avoided going back through the offices of the Police Judiciaire. He came out onto the Quai des Orfèvres in the rain, lifted the collar of his coat, walked towards the Pont Saint-Michel and had to hold out his arm a dozen times before a taxi stopped.

'Place Blanche. Corner of Rue Lepic.'

He wasn't in a good mood. He felt displeased with himself and the way the investigation was going. He was particularly upset with Philippe Liotard, who had forced him to abandon his usual methods and set all the departments in motion right from the start.

Now there were too many people dealing with the case, and he couldn't control them personally. It was all becoming far too complicated, with new protagonists emerging about whom he knew very little and whose role he was incapable of figuring out.

Twice he had felt like starting the investigation all over again, slowly, heavily, in accordance with his preferred method, but that was no longer possible. The machine had been started up and there was no way to stop it.

He would have liked, for instance, to question the concierge again, and the cobbler opposite, and the old lady on the fourth floor. But what would have been the point? Everyone had questioned them by now: inspectors, reporters, amateur detectives, people on the street. Their statements had appeared in the newspapers and they had to stand by them. It was like a track that fifty people had already trodden thoroughly.

'Do you think that bookbinder's a murderer, Monsieur Maigret?'

It was the driver, who had recognized him and was now addressing him in a familiar manner.

'I don't know.'

'If I were you, I'd concentrate on the little boy. As far as I'm concerned, he's the right lead, and I'm not just saying that because I have a child his age.'

Even the taxi-drivers were joining in! He got off at the corner of Rue Lepic and went into the bar on the corner to have a drink. The rain was dripping in big drops from the awning over the terrace, where a number of women stood frozen as if in a wax museum. He knew most of them. Some probably took their clients to the Hôtel Beauséjour.

There was a fat one outside the hotel itself, obstructing the doorway, and she smiled at him, thinking that he was coming for her, then recognized him and apologized.

He climbed the dimly lit stairs, found the owner in her office, dressed this time in black silk, with gold-rimmed glasses, her hair flaming red.

'Sit down. Will you excuse me a moment?' She went and shouted up the stairs, 'A towel for number 17, Emma!' She came back. 'Have you found anything?'

'I'd like you to have a good look at these photographs.'

He first handed her the few women's photographs selected by Moers. She looked at them one by one, shaking her head each time, then gave him back the packet.

'No. That's not the type at all. She's a bit more distinguished than those. Not so much distinguished, more "respectable", know what I mean? She looks like a decent young woman. The ones you're showing me could be my customers.'

'What about these?'

The dark-haired men. Again, she shook her head.

'No. That's not it at all. I don't know if I can explain myself. These men look too much like wops. Monsieur Levine could have stayed in a big hotel on the Champs-Élysées and nobody would have turned a hair.'

'And these?' With a sigh, he handed her the last packet.

As soon as she saw the third photograph, she froze and gave Maigret a shifty look, as if uncertain whether or not to speak.

'Is it him?'

'Maybe. Let me get closer to the light.'

A girl was climbing the stairs with a client who kept himself to the dark part of the staircase.

'Take number 7, Clémence. The room's just been done.'

She shifted her glasses on her nose.

'I could swear it's him, yes. It's a pity he's not moving. Seeing him walk, even from the back, I'd recognize him immediately. Even so, I don't think I'm wrong.'

Behind the photograph, Moers had written a summary of the man's career. Maigret was interested to discover that he was probably Belgian, like the bookbinder. Probably, because he was known by several different names and his true identity had never been established.

'I'm very grateful to you.'

'I hope you'll give me credit for this. I could have pretended not to recognize him. After all, these might be dangerous people and I'm taking a big risk.'

She was wearing so much scent, and the smells of the hotel were so persistent, that he was happy to find himself back out on the pavement, breathing in the scent of the streets in the rain.

It wasn't yet seven o'clock. Young Lapointe must have gone to see his sister to tell her, as Maigret had advised, what had happened at the Quai des Orfèvres during the day.

He was a good boy, still too nervous, too emotional, but they'd probably make something of him. Lucas, in his office, was still playing the orchestral conductor, linked by telephone to all the departments, to all the corners of Paris and elsewhere where the trio were being sought.

As for Janvier, he was still following Alfonsi, who had gone back to Rue de Turenne and had spent nearly an hour in the basement with Fernande.

Maigret had another glass of beer, during which time he read Moers' notes, which reminded him of something.

Alfred Moss, Belgian nationality (?). Approximately forty-two years old. Was a variety performer for about ten years. Belonged to a troupe of acrobats called Moss, Jef and Joe.

Maigret remembered them. He particularly remembered the one who'd been the clown: black clothes that were too big for him, never-ending shoes, a blue chin, a huge mouth, a green wig.

The man had seemed completely double-jointed, and after every acrobatic stunt he had fallen so badly, to all appearances, that it seemed impossible he hadn't broken something.

Worked in most countries of Europe and even in the United States, where he was with the Barnum Circus for four years. Abandoned this profession after an accident.

There followed the names by which the police had known him subsequently: Mosselaer, Van Vlanderen, Paterson, Smith, Thomas . . . He had been arrested successively in London, Manchester, Brussels, Amsterdam, and three or four times in Paris.

But he had never been convicted, for lack of evidence. Whichever identity he used, his papers were invariably in order and he spoke four or five languages fluently enough to change nationality as he wished.

The first time he had been investigated by the police

was in London, where he passed himself off as a Swiss citizen and worked as an interpreter in a luxury hotel. A jewellery case had disappeared from a suite he had been seen leaving, but the owner of the jewellery, an elderly American woman, testified that it was she who had called him to her suite to get him to translate a letter she had received from Germany.

Four years later, in Amsterdam, he had been suspected of a confidence trick. But this time too, the evidence had been lacking, and he had disappeared from circulation for a while.

Subsequently, the police intelligence service in Paris had taken an interest in him, at a time when there was large-scale gold smuggling across borders and Moss, now Joseph Thomas, was shuttling back and forth between France and Belgium. Again, nothing could be pinned on him.

He'd had his highs and lows, sometimes living in first-class hotels, even luxury ones, sometimes in seedy rooming houses.

For three years, nobody had seen him. Nobody knew in which country, or under which name, he was operating, if he was still operating.

Maigret walked to the phone booth and called Lucas.

'Go up and see Moers and ask him for what he's got on a man named Moss . . . Yes. Tell him he's one of the people we're looking for. He'll give you his description and the rest. Put out a general appeal. But he isn't to be arrested. In fact if we do find him, we must try not to alert him. Got that?'

'Got it, chief. There's just been another report about the boy.'

'Where?'

'Avenue Denfert-Rochereau. I sent someone. I'm waiting to hear. I'm running out of men. There was also a call from Gare du Nord. Torrence has gone there.'

He felt like walking a little in the rain, and as he passed Place d'Anvers he glanced into the park and saw the bench, streaming with water right now, where Madame Maigret had waited. Opposite, on the building at the corner of Avenue Trudaine, was a sign with the word Dentist on it in large pale letters.

He'd be back. There were lots he wanted to do but which, in the rush of things, he was always forced to put off until tomorrow.

He jumped on a bus. When he got to his door, he was surprised not to hear any noise in the kitchen and not to smell any food. He went in, crossed the dining room, where the table had not been laid, and at last saw Madame Maigret, in her slip, busy taking off her stockings.

This was so unlike her that he could find nothing to say, and when she saw him standing there wide-eyed, she burst out laughing.

'You're angry, Maigret.'

There was an unfamiliar, almost aggressive good humour in her voice. He noticed her best dress and hat on the bed.

'You'll have to make do with a cold dinner. Just imagine, I've been so busy, I haven't had time to make anything. Besides, it's so rare for you to come home for meals these days!' Sitting in the wing chair, she massaged her feet with a sigh of satisfaction. 'I don't think I've walked so much in my life!'

He just stood there, in his overcoat, with his wet hat on his head, looking at her and waiting, and she deliberately made him wait.

'I started with the department stores, although I was almost certain there was no point. But you never know, and I didn't want to blame myself later for being neglectful. Then I did the whole of Rue La Fayette, came back up Rue Notre-Dame-de-Lorette and walked along Rue Blanche and Rue de Clichy. I came back down towards the Opéra, all on foot, even when it started raining. I should mention I'd already done the Ternes and the Champs-Élysées yesterday, without telling you.

'Just to set my mind at rest, because I was sure it was going to be too expensive in those areas.'

He at last uttered the words she had been waiting for, the words she'd been trying to provoke for some time now: 'What were you looking for?'

'The hat, of course! Hadn't you got that? The business of the hat was bothering me. I didn't think it was a job for men. A tailored suit is a tailored suit, especially a blue tailored suit. But a hat, now that's different, and I'd had a good look at that one. White hats have been in fashion for some weeks now. But one hat is never exactly the same as another. Don't you see? Does it bother you to have a cold meal? I brought some things from the Italian delicatessen, Parma ham, mushrooms in vinegar, and a whole lot of little ready-made hors-d'œuvres.'

'What about the hat?'

'So now you're interested, Maigret? By the way, yours is dripping on the carpet. You really ought to take it off.'

She had succeeded, because otherwise she wouldn't have been in such a teasing mood and wouldn't have allowed herself to play with him like this. It was better to let her get on with it, and to keep his grumpy air, because she liked it.

As she was putting on a woollen dress, he sat down on the edge of the bed.

'I knew perfectly well it wasn't a hat from one of the top milliners, so there was no point looking in Rue de la Paix, Rue Saint-Honoré or Avenue Matignon. Besides, in those shops, they don't put anything in the windows and I'd have had to go in and pretend to be a customer. Can you see me trying on hats at Caroline Reboux or Rose Valois?

'But it wasn't a hat from the Galeries or Printemps either.

'Something in the middle. Still a hat by a milliner, and a fairly good milliner.

'That was why I did all the little shops, especially around Place d'Anvers, anyway not too far from there.

'I must have seen about a hundred white hats, but it was a pearl grey hat that caught my attention in the end, at Hélène et Rosine in Rue Caumartin.

'It was exactly the same, but in another colour. I was sure I was right. I told you that the hat the woman with the little boy was wearing had a very small veil, two or three centimetres wide, falling just over her eyes.

'The grey hat had the same thing.'

'Did you go in?'

Maigret had to make an effort not to smile, because this

had to be the first time the shy Madame Maigret had involved herself in a case, probably also the first time that she'd been into a milliner's shop in the Opéra area.

'Does that surprise you? You think I'm too much of an old lady? Yes, I went in. I was afraid it might be shut. I asked as naturally as I could if they had the same kind of hat in white.

'The lady said no, they had it in pale blue, in yellow, and in jade green. They had had it in white, but she'd sold it more than a month ago.'

'What did you do?' he asked, intrigued.

'I took a deep breath and said, "That's the one I saw a friend of mine wearing."

'I could see myself in the mirrors, because there are mirrors all around the shop, and my face was crimson.

'"So you know the Countess Panetti?" she asked. She was so surprised, it wasn't very flattering.

'"I've met her. I'd really like to see her again, because I've got hold of a piece of information she asked me for and I've mislaid her address."

'"I suppose she's still . . ."

'She almost stopped. She didn't completely trust me. But she didn't dare not finish her sentence.

'"I suppose she's still at Claridge's . . ."'

Madame Maigret was looking at him, at once triumphant and sardonic, with an anxious quivering of the lips despite everything.

'I hope you didn't go to Claridge's and question the doorman?' he grunted, playing the game to the end.

'No, I came straight home. Are you angry?'

'No.'

'I've already given you enough bother with this business. That's why I wanted to help you. Now come and eat, because I hope you're going to take time to have a bite before going over there.'

This dinner reminded him of their first meals as a married couple, when she had been discovering Paris and was awestruck by all the little ready-made dishes available from the Italian shops. It was more a light supper than a dinner.

'Do you think the information is good?'

'Provided you didn't get the wrong hat.'

'No, I'm certain of that. About the shoes, I wasn't so confident.'

'What's all this about shoes?'

'When you're sitting on a park bench, you naturally have your neighbour's shoes in front of your eyes. Once, when I was taking a closer look at them, I saw she was uncomfortable and tried to put her feet under the bench.'

'Why?'

'I'm going to explain, Maigret. Don't look at me like that. It isn't your fault if you don't understand anything about women's things. Suppose a woman used to the best dressmakers wants to look like an ordinary middle-class woman and not be noticed? She buys a ready-made suit, which is easy. She can also buy herself a hat which isn't a particularly luxurious one, although I'm not so sure about the hat.'

'What do you mean?'

'I mean she already had it, but thought it was similar enough to all the other white hats young women are wearing this season. She can take off her jewellery, that's no problem. But there's one thing she'll find it hard to get used to: ready-made shoes. When you get your shoes from top bootmakers, it makes your feet delicate. You've heard me moaning often enough to know that women naturally have sensitive feet. Which means she keeps her shoes, thinking they won't be noticed. That's a mistake, because I, for one, always look at the shoes first. Usually, it's the opposite that happens: you see pretty, well-dressed women, in expensive dresses or fur coats, wearing cheap shoes.'

'So you're saying she had expensive shoes?'

'Made to measure shoes, definitely. I don't know enough about the subject to know what bootmaker they came from. Other women would certainly be able to tell you.'

After eating, he took the time to pour himself a glass of sloe gin and smoke almost a whole pipe.

'Are you going to Claridge's? You won't be back too late, will you?'

He took a taxi to the Champs-Élysées, got out opposite the hotel and headed straight for the porter's office. The night porter, a man he'd known for years, was already on duty, which was an advantage, because night porters usually know more about the guests than day ones.

His arrival in a place like this always had the same effect. He could see the receptionists, the assistant manager and even the lift operator frowning and wondering what was wrong. Nobody in a luxury hotel likes a scandal, and the presence of an inspector from the Police Judiciaire is rarely a good omen.

'How are you, Benoît?'

'Not bad, Monsieur Maigret. The Americans are starting to tip.'

'Is the Countess Panetti still staying here?'

'She left at least a month ago. Would you like me to check the exact date?'

'Was her family with her?'

'What family?'

It was a quiet hour. Most of the guests were out, at the theatre or at dinner. In the gilded light, the page boys stood by the marble columns, their arms dangling, watching Maigret from a distance: they all knew him by sight.

'I never knew she had a family. She's been coming here for years and—'

'Tell me something. Have you ever seen the countess in a white hat?'

'Definitely. She got one a few days before she left.'

'Did she also wear a blue tailored suit?'

'No. You're getting mixed up, Monsieur Maigret. The one in the blue suit was her maid, or lady's companion or whatever, anyway the young lady who travels with her.'

'You've never seen the Countess Panetti in a blue suit?'

'If you knew her, you wouldn't ask me that.'

On the off-chance, Maigret showed him the women's photographs selected by Moers. 'Do any of these look like her?'

Benoît looked at Maigret in astonishment. 'Are you sure you're not making a mistake? You're showing me pictures of women who aren't even thirty, but the countess can't be far off seventy. You should ask your colleagues in the vice squad, they must know her.

'We see all kinds here. Well, the countess is one of our most eccentric guests.'

'First of all, do you know who she is?'

'She's the widow of Count Panetti, an Italian industrial-ist, big in munitions.

'She lives all over the place, in Paris, Cannes, Egypt. I think she also spends a season in Vichy every year.'

'Does she drink?'

'She drinks champagne like water, I wouldn't be sur-prised if she cleans her teeth with Pommery brut! She dresses like a young girl, makes up like a doll, and spends most of her nights in cabarets.'

'What about her maid?'

'I don't know her very well. She changes them a lot. I only saw this one this year. Last year, she had a tall redhead, a mas-seuse by profession, because she has a massage every day.'

'Do you know the latest one's name?'

'Gloria something. I don't have her form any more, but they'll tell you at the office. I don't know if she's Italian or just from the south. Toulouse, maybe?'

'Short, with brown hair?'

'Yes, elegant, pleasant, pretty. I didn't see that much of her. She didn't have a servant's room, but lived in the suite and had her meals with her mistress.'

'No men?'

'Just the son-in-law, who came to see them from time to time.'

'When?'

'Not long before they left. You'll have to ask reception for the dates. He didn't live in the hotel.'

'Do you know his name?'

'Krynker, I think. He's Czech or Hungarian.'

'Brown hair, quite fat, about forty?'

'No, nothing like that. Much younger, with very fair hair. Only just thirty, I'd say.'

They were interrupted by a group of Americans in evening dress who were handing in their keys and asking for a taxi.

'As for whether he really was her son-in-law . . .'

'Did she have affairs?'

'I don't know. I can't say yes or no.'

'Did the son-in-law ever spend the night here?'

'No. But they went out together several times.'

'With the maid?'

'She never went out in the evening with the countess. I never even saw her dressed up.'

'Do you know where they went after they left here?'

'To London, if my memory serves me well. Hold on, though. I've just remembered something. Ernest! Come here. Don't be afraid. Didn't the Countess Panetti leave her big luggage?'

'Yes, sir.'

'When our guests have to be away for a while,' Benoît explained, 'they sometimes leave some of their luggage here. We have a special store room for it. The countess left her trunks there.'

'Did she say when she'd be back?'

'Not as far as I know.'

'Did she leave alone?'

'With her maid.'

'In a taxi?'

'For that you'd have to ask the day porter. He'll be here tomorrow from eight o'clock.'

Maigret took the photograph of Moss from his pocket.

The porter merely glanced at it and grimaced. 'You won't find him here.'

'Do you know him?'

'Paterson. I knew him by the name Mosselaer when I was working in Milan about fifteen years ago. He's on file in all the big hotels and doesn't dare show up in them any more. He knows he wouldn't be given a room, wouldn't even be allowed to cross the lobby.'

'Have you seen him lately?'

'No. If I met him, I'd start by asking him to give me back the hundred lire he borrowed from me once and never gave back.'

'Does your day colleague have a phone?'

'You can always try to call him at his home in Saint-Cloud, but he doesn't often answer. He doesn't like to be disturbed in the evening and usually takes the phone off the hook.'

But he did answer. Music could be heard from the radio in the background.

'The head porter might tell you more. I don't remember calling her a taxi. Usually, when she leaves the hotel, I'm the one who gets the coach or plane tickets.'

'You didn't do that this time?'

'Now that I come to think of it, no. Maybe she left in a private car.'

'You don't know if her son-in-law, Krynker, had a car?'

'Oh, yes. A big chocolate-brown American car.'

'Many thanks. I'll probably see you tomorrow morning.'

He went over to reception, where the assistant manager, in a black jacket and striped trousers, insisted on personally looking through the records.

'She left the hotel on the evening of February 16th. I have her bill right here.'

'Was she alone?'

'I see two lunches that day. She must have eaten with her maid.'

'Can you let me have that bill?'

The bill would show the daily expenses the countess had incurred while at the hotel, and Maigret wanted to study it at his leisure.

'Provided you give it back to me! Otherwise we'll have problems with the tax people. By the way, why are the police investigating someone like the Countess Panetti?'

Preoccupied, Maigret almost replied: because of my wife!

He caught himself in time and grunted, 'I don't know yet. Something to do with a hat.'

6. The Vert-Galant Laundry Boat

Maigret walked through the revolving door and saw the garlands of lights on the Champs-Élysées. In the rain, they had always made him think of tear-stained eyes. He was getting ready to walk towards the Rond-Point when he frowned. There against the trunk of a tree, beside a flower seller sheltering from the rain, Janvier stood looking at him with a pitiful, comical air, as if trying to tell him something.

Maigret walked over to him.

'What are you doing here?'

Janvier pointed to a figure silhouetted against one of the few lighted shop windows. It was Alfonsi, who seemed to be taking a great interest in a display of trunks.

'He's been following you. Which means I've been following you too.'

'Did he see Liotard after his visit to Rue de Turenne?'

'No. He phoned him.'

'Call it a day. Can I give you a lift home?'

Janvier lived in Rue Réaumur, almost on Maigret's route.

Alfonsi watched them both leaving. He looked surprised and disconcerted. Then, as Maigret hailed a taxi, he made up his mind, turned and walked away in the direction of the Étoile.

'Anything new?'

'Lots. Almost too much.'

'Do you want me to keep tailing Alfonsi tomorrow morning?'

'No. Drop by the office. There'll probably be work for everyone.'

Once Janvier had got out, Maigret said to the driver, 'Go via Rue de Turenne.'

It wasn't late. He was vaguely hoping the lights would be on at the bookbinder's. This would have been the ideal moment to have a long talk with Fernande, as he'd been wanting to do for a long time.

Seeing a reflection on the window, he got out of the taxi, but then he noticed that everything was dark inside, hesitated to knock, and set off again for the Quai des Orfèvres, where he found Torrence on duty and gave him some instructions.

Madame Maigret had just got into bed when he tiptoed into the room. As he undressed in the dark, in order not to wake her, she asked, 'What about the hat?'

'It was definitely bought by the Countess Panetti.'

'Did you see her?'

'No. But she's about seventy-five.'

He went to bed in a bad mood, preoccupied, and not only was it still raining when he woke up, he then cut himself shaving.

'Are you continuing with your investigation?' he asked his wife as she served him his breakfast with her hair in curlers.

'Do I have anything else to do?' she said, straight-faced.

'I don't know. Now that you've started . . .'

He bought a newspaper at the corner of Boulevard Voltaire. There was no new statement from Philippe Liotard, no new challenge. The night porter at Claridge's had been discreet, because there was no mention of the countess either.

At the Quai, Lucas had received his instructions when relieving Torrence, and the machine was already in full swing. Now they were looking for the Italian countess on the Riviera and in foreign capitals, while simultaneously taking an interest in Krynker and the maid.

On the platform of the bus in the drizzle, a traveller opposite Maigret was reading a newspaper, with a headline that gave the inspector food for thought.

The investigation is getting nowhere

How many people were dealing with it at this very hour? They were still watching the stations, the ports, the airports. They were still searching hotels and rooming houses, they were trying to track down Alfred Moss not only in Paris, not only in France, but in London, Brussels, Amsterdam and Rome.

Maigret walked along Rue de Turenne, went into the Tabac des Vosges to buy a packet of shag and took the opportunity to have a glass of white wine. There were no reporters, but only local people who were starting to become disenchanted.

The bookbinder's door was closed. He knocked, soon saw Fernande emerge from the basement by the spiral staircase – in curlers, like Madame Maigret. She hesitated when she recognized him through the window, but then came and opened the door.

'I'd like to talk to you for a moment.'

It was cold on the staircase, because the stove hadn't been lit.

'Do you prefer to go downstairs?'

He followed her into the kitchen, which she had been busy cleaning when he had disturbed her.

She seemed tired too, with a kind of discouragement in her eyes.

'Would you like a cup of coffee? I have some made.'

He accepted and sat down at the table. She eventually sat down opposite him, pulling the edges of her dressing gown together across her bare legs.

'Alfonsi came to see you again yesterday. What does he want?'

'I don't know. He's mainly interested in the questions you ask me. He says I shouldn't trust you.'

'Did you tell him about the attempted poisoning?'

'Yes.'

'Why?'

'You didn't tell me to keep quiet. I can't remember how it came into the conversation. He's working for Liotard, so it's natural he should know these things.'

'Have you had any other visitors?'

He had the impression she hesitated, but it may have been the effect of the exhaustion afflicting her. She had poured herself a full bowl of coffee. She must have been drinking a lot of black coffee to keep going.

'No. None at all.'

'Did you tell your husband why you weren't bringing him his meals any more?'

'I had a chance to warn him. Thanks for that.'

'Has anybody phoned you?'

'I don't think so. I sometimes hear the phone ring. But by the time I get upstairs, there's nobody on the line.'

He took the photograph of Alfred Moss from his pocket. 'Do you know this man?'

She looked at the photograph, then at Maigret, and said quite naturally, 'Of course.'

'Who is he?'

'Alfred, my husband's brother.'

'Have you seen him recently?'

'I almost never see him. Sometimes, more than a year goes by without his coming here. He lives abroad most of the time.'

'Do you know what he does?'

'Not exactly. Frans says he's a loser, a failure, someone who's never had any luck.'

'Has he ever talked to you about his profession?'

'I know he used to work in a circus, that he was an acrobat, and that he fell and broke his spine.'

'And since then?'

'Isn't he some kind of impresario?'

'You know he doesn't call himself Steuvels like his brother, but Moss? Do you have any idea why?'

'Yes.'

She seemed reluctant to continue. She looked at the photograph Maigret had left on the kitchen table, near the coffee bowls, then stood up to switch off the gas under the pan of water.

'I suppose I guessed most of it. Maybe if you asked Frans about it he'd tell you more. You know his parents were very poor, but that's not the whole truth. In fact, his mother did the same work I used to, in Ghent, or rather in some dubious suburb of the town.

'On top of that, she drank. I suspect she may have been half mad. She had seven or eight children, but in most cases didn't know who their fathers were.

'It was Frans who chose the name Steuvels later. His mother's name was Mosselaer.'

'Is she dead?'

'I think so. He doesn't like to talk about her.'

'Has he kept in touch with his brothers and sisters?'

'I don't think so. Alfred is the only one who comes to see him from time to time, but not very often. He must have his highs and lows. Sometimes he seems prosperous, he's well dressed, comes here in a taxi, brings gifts. At other times he's quite shabby.'

'When was the last time you saw him?'

'Let me see now. It must have been at least two months ago.'

'Did he stay for dinner?'

'Yes, as usual.'

'Tell me, during these visits, did your husband ever try to send you out of the house for any reason?'

'No. Why should he? They sometimes stayed alone in the workshop, but from downstairs, where I was cooking, it was easy to hear what they were saying.'

'What did they talk about?'

'Nothing in particular. Moss liked to reminisce about the time when he was an acrobat and the countries where he's lived. He was almost always the one who referred to their childhood and their mother, that's how I know about it.'

'Alfred is the younger of the two, I assume?'

'By three or four years. Afterwards, Frans would sometimes walk him to the corner of the street. That's the only time I wasn't with them.'

'Did they ever talk business?'

'No, never.'

'Did Alfred ever come with friends, women friends for example?'

'I always saw him alone. I think he was married once. I'm not sure. I have a feeling he mentioned it. He was in love with a woman, but it didn't work out well.'

It was quiet and warm in this little kitchen, from where you could see nothing of the outside world and where it was necessary to keep the light on all day. Maigret would have liked to have Frans Steuvels there in front of him and talk to him as he was talking to his wife.

'You told me when I was last here that he almost never went out without you. But he did go to the bank from time to time.'

'I don't call that going out. It's just round the corner. All he had to do was cross Place des Vosges.'

'And apart from that, you were together from morning till night?'

'Pretty much. I'd go out shopping of course, but always locally. Once in a blue moon, I might go into the centre of town to buy something. I don't care much about my appearance, as you may have noticed.'

'You never went to see your family?'

'I only have my mother and sister in Concarneau. It was only because of that fake telegram that I visited them.'

It was as if something was bothering Maigret. 'There wasn't a set day for you to go out?'

On her side, she seemed to be making an effort to think about that and give him an answer. 'No. Apart from wash day, obviously.'

'So you don't do your washing here?'

'Where would I do it? I have to go upstairs to fetch water. I can't hang clothes to dry in the workshop and they wouldn't dry in the basement. Once a week, in summer, and once every two weeks in winter, I go to the laundry boat on the Seine.'

'Where?'

'Square du Vert-Galant. You know, just below the Pont-Neuf. It takes me half a day. The next day, I go and pick up the washing. By then, it's dry and ready to iron.'

Maigret was visibly relaxing, smoking his pipe with more pleasure, and with a gleam in his eyes. 'So one day a week in summer, and one day a fortnight in winter, Frans was alone here?'

'Not all day.'

'Did you go to the laundry boat in the morning or in the afternoon?'

'In the afternoon. I tried going there in the morning, but it was difficult, because of the housework and the cooking.'

'Did you have a key to the house?'

'Of course.'

'Have you often had to use it?'

'What do you mean?'

'Did you ever come back and not find your husband in the workshop?'

'Very seldom.'

'But it has happened?'

'I think so. Yes.'

'Recently?'

It seemed to have only just occurred to her, and she hesitated. 'The week I left for Concarneau.'

'Which is your washing day?'

'Monday.'

'Did he get back a long time after you?'

'Not long. Maybe an hour.'

'Did you ask him where he'd been?'

'I never ask him anything. He's free. It's not up to me to ask him questions.'

'You don't know if he'd left the neighbourhood? You weren't worried?'

'I was in the doorway when he got back. I saw him get off the bus at the corner of Rue des Francs-Bourgeois.'

'The bus from the centre or from the Bastille?'

'From the centre.'

'As far as I can judge from this photograph, the two brothers seem to be the same height. Is that right?'

'Yes. Alfred looks thinner, because he has a thin face, but his body's more muscular. They don't look alike, except that they both have red hair. From the back, though, the resemblance is striking, and I've even mistaken one for the other.'

'The times you saw Alfred, how was he dressed?'

'It depended, as I already said.'

'Do you think he ever borrowed money from his brother?'

'I thought about that, but I don't think it's likely. He certainly never did it in front of me.'

'The last time he came, was he wearing a blue suit?'

She looked him in the eyes. She had understood. 'I'm almost sure he was wearing dark clothes, more grey than blue. When you live with the lights on all the time, you stop noticing colours.'

'How did you and your husband deal with money?'

'What do you mean?'

'Did he give you housekeeping money every month?'

'No. Whenever I was short, I'd ask him for more.'

'Did he ever object?'

She blushed slightly. 'He was absent-minded. He always thought he'd given me money the day before. So he'd be surprised and say, "Again?"'

'What about your personal things, your dresses, your hats?'

'You know, I spend very little!'

Now she started asking him questions, as if she had waited a long time for this moment.

'Listen, inspector, I'm not very intelligent, but I'm not stupid either. You've questioned me, your inspectors have questioned me, and so have the reporters, not to mention the suppliers and the local people. A young man of seventeen who likes to think he's an amateur detective even stopped me in the street and read out prepared questions from a little notebook.

'Before anything else, answer me honestly: do you believe Frans is guilty?'

'Guilty of what?'

'You know perfectly well: killing a man and burning the body in the stove.'

He hesitated. He could have told her all kinds of things, but he was determined to be sincere. 'I have no idea.'

'Then why keep him in prison?'

'Firstly, it's not up to me, it's up to the examining magistrate. Secondly, we can't lose sight of the fact that all the material evidence points to him.'

'The teeth!' she retorted ironically.

'And especially the bloodstains on the blue suit. And don't forget the suitcase that disappeared.'

'Which I never saw!'

'It doesn't matter. Other people saw it, a police inspector at least. There's also the fact that, as if by chance, you'd been called away to the provinces at that particular moment by a fake telegram. Just between ourselves, I can tell you that if it was up to me, I'd rather your husband was free, but for his own good I'd be wary of releasing him. You saw what happened yesterday?'

'Yes. That's what I'm thinking of.'

'Whether he's guilty or innocent, it seems there are people who want him out of the way.'

'Why did you show me his brother's photograph?'

'Because contrary to what you might think, his brother is quite a dangerous villain.'

'Has he killed someone?'

'Unlikely. That kind of person seldom kills. But he's wanted by the police in three or four countries, and for more than fifteen years now he's been making his living by theft and fraud. Does that surprise you?'

'No.'

'So it had already crossed your mind?'

'When Frans told me his brother was unfortunate, I had the feeling he wasn't using the word unfortunate in its usual sense. Do you think Alfred would have been capable of kidnapping a child?'

'Once again, I have to say I have no idea. By the way, have you ever heard of the Countess Panetti?'

'Who's she?'

'A wealthy Italian woman who was staying at Claridge's.'

'Has she also been killed?'

'It's possible, just as it's possible she's simply spending the carnival season in Cannes or Nice. I'll know this evening. I'd like to take another look at your husband's account books.'

'Come upstairs. I have lots of questions to ask you, but I can't think of them right now. It's when you're not here that I think about them. I should write them down, like that young man who thinks he's a detective.'

She let him go ahead of her up the stairs, then went to a shelf and took down a large black book the police had already examined five or six times.

At the end of it, there was an alphabetical list of the bookbinder's old and new customers. The name Panetti wasn't on it. Nor was Krynker.

Steuvels had small, irregular handwriting, with letters that overlapped and an unusual way of forming rs and ts.

'Have you ever heard the name Krynker?'

'Not as far as I recall. We were together all day, you know, but I never felt I had the right to ask him questions. You seem sometimes to forget, inspector, that I'm not a woman like any other. Remember where he found me. I was always surprised by what he did. It suddenly occurs to me that the reason he did it was because he was thinking about what his mother had been.'

As if he hadn't been listening, Maigret walked with large strides to the door, opened it abruptly and caught Alfonsi by the collar of his camelhair coat.

'Come here, you. So you're at it again. Have you decided to spend your days tailing me?'

Alfonsi tried to brazen it out, but Maigret tightened his grip, shaking him like a puppet.

'Do you mind telling me what you're doing here?'

'I was waiting for you to leave.'

'So that you could harass this woman?'

'I have a right to be here. As long as she agrees to see me . . .'

'What are you looking for?'

'Ask Maître Liotard.'

'Liotard or no Liotard, I warn you of one thing: the next time I find you following me, I'll have you put away for living off immoral earnings, got that?'

It wasn't an idle threat. Maigret was not unaware that the woman Alfonsi lived with spent most of her nights in the cabarets of Montmartre and had no hesitation in taking passing strangers to hotels.

When he turned back to Fernande, he looked relieved. Alfonsi could be seen hurrying towards Place des Vosges in the rain.

'What kind of questions does he ask?'

'Always the same. He wants to know what you've been asking me, what I've replied, what you're interested in, what things here you've examined.'

'I think he'll leave you alone from now on.'

'Do you think Maître Liotard is harming my husband?'

'The way things are now, I think we just have to let him carry on.'

He had to go back downstairs, because he had left the photograph of Moss on the kitchen table. Instead of going back to the Quai des Orfèvres, he crossed the road and went into the cobbler's shop.

It was only nine in the morning, but the cobbler had already had a few drinks and smelled of white wine.

'Hard at work, inspector?'

The two shops were directly opposite each other. The cobbler and the bookbinder couldn't help but see each other when they looked out, each bent over his work, with just the width of the street between them.

'Do you remember any of Steuvels' customers?'

'A few, yes.'

'This one?'

He showed him the photograph. Fernande was watching them anxiously from across the street.

'I call him the clown.'

'Why?'

'I don't know. Because I think he looks like a clown.' All at once, he scratched his head and seemed to make a welcome discovery. 'Look, buy me a drink and I think I can give you your money's worth. It's a stroke of luck you showed me that picture. I mentioned the word clown and I suddenly thought of a suitcase. Why? Oh yes! Because clowns usually come into the ring with a suitcase.'

'Not the acrobatic ones.'

'Clown, acrobat, it's all the same. How about that drink?'

'Afterwards.'

'Don't you trust me? You're making a mistake. Straight as a die, that's what I always say. This fellow of yours is definitely the man with the suitcase.'

'What man with the suitcase?'

The cobbler gave him what was intended as a knowing wink. 'You're not going to try and outsmart me, are you? Don't I read the newspapers? And what did the newspapers keep talking about when this all started? Didn't they come and ask me if I'd seen Frans or his wife or anyone else leave with a suitcase?'

'You saw the man in the photograph leave with a suitcase?'

'Not that day. I didn't notice anyway. No, I'm thinking about the other times.'

'Did he come often?'

'Yes, quite often.'

'Once a week, for instance? Or once a fortnight?

'It's possible. I don't want to make anything up, because

I don't know the grilling the lawyers will give me the day the case goes to trial. I'd just say he came often.'

'In the morning or the afternoon?'

'I think the afternoon. You know why? Because I remember seeing him when the lights were on, so it must have been the afternoon. He always arrived with a little suitcase.'

'Brown?'

'Probably. Aren't most suitcases brown? He'd sit down in a corner of the workshop, wait for the work to be finished, and leave with the suitcase.'

'Was he there long?'

'I don't know. Definitely more than an hour. Sometimes I had the feeling he stayed there all afternoon.'

'Did he come on a particular day?'

'That I don't know either.'

'Think before you answer. Did you ever see this man in the workshop at the same time as Madame Steuvels?'

'At the same time as Fernande? Wait. I can't quite remember. I do remember the two men left together once, and Frans closed his shop.'

'Recently?'

'I'd have to think about that. When are we going for our drink?'

Maigret was forced to go with him to the Grand Turenne, where the cobbler assumed a triumphant air.

'Two old marcs. He's paying!'

He drank three, one after the other, and was about to repeat his story about the clown when Maigret managed to get away from him. As he passed the bookbinder's workshop, Fernande gave him a reproachful look through the window.

But he had to carry out his task to the end. He went into the concierge's lodge. She was busy peeling potatoes.

'Oh, so you're back in the neighbourhood!' she said sharply, upset that she had been neglected for so long.

'Do you know this man?'

She went to a drawer to get her glasses.

'I don't know his name, if that's what you want, but I've seen him before. Didn't the cobbler tell you what you wanted to know?'

She was jealous that others had been questioned before her.

'Have you seen him often?'

'I've seen him, that's all I know.'

'Was he a customer of the bookbinder's?'

'I suppose so, because he came to his shop.'

'Did he come on other occasions?'

'I think he sometimes had dinner with them, but I don't stick my nose into my tenants' affairs!'

The stationer's opposite, the cardboard factory, the umbrella shop: it became routine, always the same question, the same gesture of producing the photograph, which people examined gravely. Some hesitated. Others had seen the man, without remembering where or in what circumstances.

As he was about to leave the neighbourhood, Maigret decided to drop into the Tabac des Vosges.

'Have you ever seen this man?'

'The man with the suitcase!' the owner said without any hesitation.

'Can you tell me more?'

'I don't know what he sells, but he probably goes door to door. He's come in here quite often, always just after lunch. He always has a strawberry syrup with Vichy water. He told me he had a stomach ulcer.'

'Did he stay for long?'

'Sometimes a quarter of an hour, sometimes longer. Oh, and he always sat in that seat, near the window.'

From where there was a view of the corner of Rue de Turenne!

'He must have had appointments with customers and was just killing time. Once, not so long ago, he sat there nearly an hour and in the end asked for a telephone token.'

'Do you know who he called?'

'No. When he came out of the booth he left immediately.'

'In what direction?'

'I didn't notice.'

As a reporter was just then coming in, the owner asked Maigret in a low voice, 'Is this on the record?'

Maigret shrugged. It was pointless to make a mystery of it, now that the cobbler knew everything. 'It's up to you.'

When he walked into Lucas' office, Lucas was juggling two telephone calls, and Maigret had to wait a while.

'I'm still looking for the countess,' Lucas sighed, mopping his brow. 'The sleeping car company, who know her well, haven't seen her on any of their lines for months. I've spoken to most of the big hotels in Cannes, Nice, Antibes and Villefranche. Not a thing. I also spoke to the casinos, but she hasn't set foot in any of them either. Right now, Lapointe, who speaks English, is calling Scotland Yard, and I can't remember who's dealing with the Italians.'

Before going to see Judge Dossin, Maigret went upstairs to say hello to Moers and give him back the photographs that hadn't led anywhere.

'No results?' poor Moers asked.

'One out of three isn't bad. We just have to get our hands on the other two, though it's possible they never had their mugshots taken.'

By midday, they still hadn't tracked down the Countess Panetti, and two Italian reporters, who had been alerted, were waiting excitedly at the door of Maigret's office.

7. Maigret's Sunday

Madame Maigret was somewhat surprised when her husband phoned her at about three o'clock on Saturday afternoon to ask if dinner was already cooking.

'Not yet. Why? . . . What's that? I'd love to, obviously. If you're sure you'll be free . . . Absolutely sure? . . . All right, then. I'll get dressed. I'll be there . . . By the clock, yes. No, no choucroute for me, but I'll happily eat a pork hotpot . . . What? You aren't joking, are you, Maigret? You are serious? Wherever I like? It's too good to be true, I bet an hour from now you're going to call me back and tell me you won't be back to eat or to sleep. Well, I'm getting ready anyway!'

So that Saturday, instead of cooking smells, the apartment on Boulevard Richard-Lenoir smelled of warm bathwater, eau de Cologne and the slightly sweet perfume that Madame Maigret kept reserved for special occasions.

Maigret was almost on time – just five minutes late, in fact – at the Alsatian restaurant in Rue d'Enghien where they sometimes had dinner and where, relaxed, apparently thinking the same thoughts as other men, he now ate a choucroute cooked just the way he liked it.

'Have you chosen the cinema?'

That was what had made Madame Maigret so incredulous on the phone earlier: he had invited her to spend the evening in whichever cinema she liked.

They went to the Paramount on Boulevard des Italiens and Maigret queued for tickets without grumbling, emptying his pipe into an enormous spittoon as they went in.

They heard the electric organ, and then the orchestra rose from ground level on a platform, while a curtain was transformed into a kind of synthetic sunset. It was only after the cartoons that Madame Maigret understood. The trailers had been and gone, followed by commercials for a sugary cereal and furniture on the instalment plan.

We are informed by the Prefecture of Police . . .

It was the first time she had seen those words on a screen. Immediately afterwards, a full-face mugshot appeared, then another in profile. It was Alfred Moss. A list of his various identities was also shown.

Anyone who has seen this man in the past two months is asked to immediately telephone . . .

'Was that why?' she said once they were out in the street, walking part of the way home in order to get some air.

'Not just because of that. Actually, it wasn't my idea. It was suggested to the Prefecture a long time ago, but this is the first time it's been done. It was Moers who pointed out that photographs published in the newspapers never look right, because of the grain, or the ink used. But if you show them on a cinema screen the fact that every-thing's enlarged makes more of an impression.'

'Well, whether it was for that or another reason, I really enjoyed myself. When was the last time we did it?'

'Three weeks ago?' he said, in all sincerity.

'Exactly two and a half months ago!'

They argued a little, just for fun. And the following morning, because of the sun, which was again bright and springlike, Maigret sang in his bath. He walked all the way to the Quai des Orfèvres, along almost deserted streets, and it was always a pleasure to find all the doors open in the wide corridors of the Police Judiciaire and most of the offices unoccupied.

Lucas had only just arrived. Torrence was there too, as was Janvier. Young Lapointe soon appeared. Because it was a Sunday, it felt as if they were working for the love of it. And maybe that was why they left the doors open between their offices. From time to time, by way of music, the bells of the nearby churches pealed out.

Lapointe was the only one who had brought in any new information. The previous day, before leaving, Maigret had asked him, 'By the way, that young reporter who's seeing your sister, where does he live?'

'You mean Antoine Bizard. He isn't seeing her anymore.'

'Have they quarrelled?'

'I don't know. Maybe he's afraid of me.'

'I'd like his address.'

'I don't know it. I know where he usually eats. I don't think my sister knows more than that. I'll find out from the newspaper.'

This morning, on arriving, he handed Maigret a piece of

paper. It was the address he had asked for: a building in Rue de Provence, the same one where Philippe Liotard lived.

'That's good, son, thank you,' Maigret simply said, without making any further comment.

If it had been a little warmer, he would have taken off his jacket and remained in his shirt-sleeves, like people who tinker on Sundays – because tinkering was precisely what he intended to do. All his pipes were laid out on his desk, and he took from his pocket the big black notebook he always filled with notes but almost never consulted.

Two or three times, he threw the large sheets he had scribbled on into the waste-paper basket. He had started by drawing columns, then changed his mind.

But in the end, his work began to take shape.

Thursday, 15 February. The Countess Panetti leaves Claridge's with her maid, Gloria Lotti, in her son-in-law Krynker's chocolate-brown Chrysler.

The date had been confirmed by the day porter. As for the car, the information had been provided by one of the hotel's valets, who had also indicated the time of departure as seven in the evening. He had added that the old woman seemed anxious and that her son-in-law was in a hurry, as if they were going to miss a train or an important appointment.

There was still no trace of the countess. He went and made sure of that in the next office, where Lucas was still receiving reports from all over.

Although the Italian reporters the previous day hadn't got much from the Police Judiciaire, they had supplied some information themselves. They both knew of the Countess Panetti. The wedding of her only daughter, Bella, had caused something of a stir in Italy, because her mother hadn't given her consent and the girl had run away from home and got married in Monte Carlo.

That was five years ago, and since then the two women had not seen each other.

'Krynker must have been in Paris to attempt another reconciliation,' the Italian reporters had said.

Friday, 16 February. Gloria Lotti, wearing the countess's white hat, goes to Concarneau. From there, she sends a telegram to Fernande Steuvels. She returns to Paris the same night without having seen anyone.

In the margin, he amused himself drawing a woman's hat with a little veil.

Saturday, 17 February. At midday, Fernande leaves Rue de Turenne to travel to Concarneau. Her husband doesn't go with her to the station. At about four o'clock, a customer comes to collect some work he has ordered, and finds Frans Steuvels in his workshop, where everything seems perfectly normal. Questioned about the suitcase, the customer doesn't recall seeing it.

At a few minutes after eight o'clock, three people, including Alfred Moss, and probably also the man who will later register in Rue Lepic under the name Levine are driven by taxi from Gare Saint-Lazare to the corner of Rue de Turenne and Rue des Francs-Bourgeois.

Just before nine o'clock, the concierge hears someone knocking at Steuvels' door. She has the impression the three men went in.

In the margin, in red pencil, he wrote: Is the third man Krynker?

Sunday, 18 February. The stove, which hasn't been lit lately, has been on all night, and Frans Steuvels has to make at least five trips to the yard to carry ashes to the dustbins.

Mademoiselle Béguin, who lives on the fourth floor, is disturbed by the smoke 'which had a strange smell'.

Monday, 19 February. The stove is still on. The bookbinder is alone at home all day.

Tuesday, 20 February. The Police Judiciaire receive an anonymous tip-off about a body having been burnt in the bookbinder's stove. Fernande returns from Concarneau.

Wednesday, 21 February. Lapointe pays a visit to Rue de Turenne. Under a table in the workshop, he sees a suitcase with a handle that has been repaired with string. Lapointe leaves the workshop about midday. He has lunch with his sister and tells her about the case. Does Mademoiselle Lapointe meet her boyfriend, Antoine Bizard, who lives in the same building as Liotard, a lawyer who doesn't have any cases? Or does she phone him?

Before five in the afternoon, Liotard goes to Rue de Turenne on the pretext of ordering an ex-libris.

By the time Lucas carries out his search at five o'clock, the suitcase has disappeared. Interrogation of Steuvels at the Police Judiciaire. Towards the end of the night, he appoints Maître Liotard as his lawyer.

Maigret went for a little walk and glanced at the notes the inspectors were taking while speaking on the phone. It wasn't time yet to have beer sent up, and he made do with filling another pipe.

Thursday, 22 February.
Friday, 23 February.
Saturday . . .

A whole column of dates, with nothing opposite, except that the investigation was getting nowhere, the newspapers were on the offensive, and Liotard, as angry as a mutt, was attacking the police in general and Maigret in particular. The right-hand column remained empty until:

Sunday, 10 March. A man named Levine takes a room at the Hôtel Beauséjour in Rue Lepic, and settles in with a young boy of about two.

Gloria Lotti, who passes for his nurse, looks after the child, taking him to Square d'Anvers every morning for a bit of air while Levine sleeps.

She does not sleep at the hotel, which she leaves late at night when Levine gets back.

Monday, 11 March. Ditto.

Tuesday, 12 March. At 9.30, Gloria and the boy leave the Hôtel Beauséjour as usual. At 9.45, Moss turns up at the hotel and asks for Levine. Levine immediately packs his bags and takes them downstairs while Moss remains alone in the room.

10.55: Gloria spots Levine and hurriedly leaves the boy in the care of Madame Maigret.

Soon after 11, Gloria and Levine get back to the Beauséjour. They find Moss there and the three of them argue for more than an hour. Moss is the first to leave. At 12.45, Gloria and Levine leave the hotel, and Gloria gets into a taxi on her own.

She returns to Square d'Anvers and collects the child.

She is driven to Porte de Neuilly, then asks to be taken to Gare Saint-Lazare. On Place Saint-Augustin, she suddenly stops the taxi and gets into another one. She gets out of this one, still with the boy, at the corner of Faubourg Montmartre and the Grands Boulevards.

The page was quite picturesque, because Maigret had decorated it with what looked like children's drawings.

On another sheet, he noted down the dates on which they had lost track of the various individuals involved.

Countess Panetti: 16 February.

The valet from Claridge's had been the last to see her, when she had got into her son-in-law's chocolate-brown Chrysler.

Krynker?

Maigret hesitated to put the date of 17 February, because there was no evidence that he was the third man dropped by the taxi at the corner of Rue de Turenne.

If it wasn't him, then he had been lost sight of at the same time as the old woman.

Alfred Moss: Tuesday, 12 March.

He had been the first to leave the Hôtel Beauséjour, at about midday.

Levine: Tuesday, 12 March.

Half an hour after Moss, as he was putting Gloria in the taxi.

Gloria and the boy: Same date.

Two hours later, in the crowd at the Carrefour Montmartre.

It was now Sunday, 17 March. Since the 12th, there had again been nothing new to report. Just the investigation.

Or rather, there was one date still to be noted down, which he added to the column:

Friday, 15 March. Someone in the Métro tries (?) to put poison in the food prepared for Frans Steuvels.

But that remained doubtful. The experts hadn't discovered any trace of poison. Given the nervous state Fernande had been in lately, she might well have misinterpreted what had simply been a passenger's clumsiness.

In any case, it couldn't have been Moss, because she would have recognized him.

Levine?

What if they hadn't been trying to put poison in the pan but leave a message there?

Maigret blinked because a ray of sunlight had struck his face, made a few more little drawings, then went to the window and looked out at a line of boats passing on the Seine and families in their Sunday best crossing the Pont Saint-Michel.

Madame Maigret must have gone back to bed, as she sometimes did on Sundays, but only to give a little more of a Sunday feeling, because she was incapable of falling asleep again.

'Janvier! How about ordering some beer?'

Janvier phoned the Brasserie Dauphine, whose owner naturally asked, 'What about sandwiches?'

Maigret made a tentative phone call and discovered that the scrupulous Judge Dossin was also at his desk, no doubt hoping, like him, to take stock of the case with a clear head.

'Still nothing on the car?'

It was funny to think that, on this beautiful Sunday that smelled of spring, conscientious gendarmes were looking at the cars parked outside village churches and cafés, in search of a chocolate-brown Chrysler.

'Can I have a look, chief?' asked Lucas, who had dropped into Maigret's office between two telephone calls. He gave Maigret's work a careful once-over and shook his head. 'Why didn't you ask me? I drew up the same chart, only more detailed.'

'But without the drawings!' Maigret joked. 'What are we getting more calls about? The car or Moss?'

'The car, for the moment. Lots of brown cars. Unfortunately, when I insist, it turns out they're not exactly chocolate, more maroon, or else they're Citroëns or Peugeots. We check them anyway. We've started getting calls from the suburbs, and they're coming in from even further away, a hundred kilometres from Paris.'

Soon, thanks to the radio, the whole of France would join in. All they could do was wait, and it wasn't so unpleasant. The waiter from the brasserie brought a huge tray covered in beers and piles of sandwiches, and there was a good chance he would make more journeys today.

They were eating and drinking and had just opened the windows, because the sun was warm, when they saw Moers come in, blinking in the light, as if emerging from a dark place.

They hadn't known he was in the house. Theoretically, he had nothing to do here today. But he had come from upstairs, where he must have been alone in the labs.

'Sorry to disturb you.'

'A glass of beer? There's one left.'

'No, thanks. I was just going to sleep last night when an idea started niggling at me. We were so sure the blue suit belonged to Steuvels that we only examined it from the point of view of the bloodstains. As it's still upstairs, I came here this morning to analyse the dust particles.'

It was the routine thing to do, but the fact was that nobody had thought of it in the present case. Moers had placed each item of clothing in a strong paper bag which he had then beaten for a long time to get even the smallest particles of dust out of the fabric.

'Did you find anything?'

'Large quantities of very fine sawdust. Actually, more like wood powder.'

'Like in a sawmill?'

'No. The particles would be less fine, less pervasive. This powder's produced by some kind of precision work.'

'Cabinet making, for instance?'

'Perhaps. I'm not sure. It's even finer than that, in my opinion, but before I come to a conclusion, I'd like to talk to the head of the lab tomorrow.'

Without waiting for the end, Janvier had grabbed a telephone directory and was studying all the addresses in Rue de Turenne.

The most varied trades were represented, some quite unexpected, but, as luck would have it, they almost all had something to do with metals or cardboard.

'I just thought I'd come and let you know. I don't know if it's of any use.'

Neither did Maigret. In a case like this, you could never predict what might be useful. But it did tend to support Frans Steuvels, who had always denied being the owner of the blue suit.

But why, then, did he have a blue coat, which didn't really match a brown suit?

The telephone! Sometimes, six phones were ringing at the same time, and the switchboard operator didn't know where to turn, because there weren't enough people available to take the calls.

'What is it?'

'Lagny.'

Maigret had been there once. It was a little town on the banks of the Marne, with lots of anglers and varnished canoes. He couldn't remember what case had taken him there, but it had been summer and he had drunk a nice little white wine, the memory of which lingered.

Lucas was taking notes, all the while signalling to Maigret that it sounded genuine.

'We may have something,' he said with a sigh as he hung up. 'That was the gendarmerie from Lagny on the phone. For a month now, they've been in a tizzy about a car that fell into the Marne.'

'It fell into the Marne a month ago?'

'From what I could understand, yes. The sergeant I had on the phone was so intent on explaining in as much detail as possible, I couldn't follow any of it by the end. Plus, he kept mentioning all these names as if I knew them, as if he was talking about Jesus Christ or Pasteur. But the one he mentioned most was old Madame Hébart or Hobart, who gets drunk every night, but who's apparently incapable of making things up.

'Anyway, this all happened about a month ago . . .'

'Did he tell you the exact date?'

'February 15th.'

Maigret consulted the chronology he'd put together, proud that it was coming in useful.

15 February. The Countess Panetti leaves Claridge's with her maid, Gloria Lotti, in her son-in-law Krynker's chocolate-brown Chrysler.

'I thought of that. Like I said, it sounds genuine. So, this old woman, who lives in an isolated house by the river and rents boats to anglers in the summer, went to have a drink in the local tavern, as she does every evening. On her way home, she claims she heard a loud noise in the darkness, and she's sure it was the noise of a car falling into the Marne.

'The water level was high at the time. There's a little path that branches off from the main road and stops at the edge of the water. It would have been muddy, and probably slippery.'

'Did she tell the gendarmerie straight away?'

'No, she mentioned it at the café the next day. The news took a while to spread. One of the gendarmes finally heard about it and questioned her.

'The gendarmes went to have a look, but the banks were partly submerged and the current was so strong that navigation had to be interrupted for several days. Apparently, it's only now that the level's getting more or less back to normal.

'Basically, I don't think they took the thing seriously at all.

'Yesterday, after getting our appeal about the brown car, they had a phone call from somebody who lives on the corner of the main road and the path, and who claims that one night last month he saw a car that colour turn in front of his house.

'He sells petrol, and was just filling up a customer's car, which explains why he was outside at that hour.'

'What time was it?'

'Just after nine.'

It doesn't take two hours to get to Lagny from the Champs-Élysées, but obviously there was nothing to stop Krynker from having made a detour.

'What happened next?'

'The gendarmerie asked the Highways Department for a crane.'

'This was yesterday?'

'Yesterday afternoon. A lot of people gathered to watch. They did hook something in the evening, but then darkness fell and they had to stop. I was even told the name of the hole, because all the holes in the riverbed are known by anglers and local people. There's even one that's ten metres deep.'

'Did they fish out the car?'

'This morning. Sure enough, it's a chocolate-brown Chrysler, with an Alpes-Maritimes licence number. That's not all. There's a body inside.'

'A man's body?'

'A woman's. It's very decomposed. Most of the clothes were torn off by the current. The hair is long and grey.'

'The Countess?'

'I don't know. They've only just found the body. It's still on the bank, under a tarpaulin, and they're asking what they should do. I told them I'd call them back.'

Moers had left a few minutes earlier. He would have been useful to Maigret right now, and there wasn't much chance they would find him at home.

'Do you want to call Dr Paul?'

Paul answered himself.

'Are you busy? Do you have any plans for today? Would you mind if I came and picked you up and took you to Lagny? With your kit, yes. No, it's not likely to be pretty. An old woman who's been in the Marne for a month.'

Maigret looked around him and saw Lapointe blush and turn his head away. He was clearly dying to go with his chief.

'Don't you have a girlfriend to see this afternoon?'

'Oh, no, sir!'

'Can you drive?'

'I've had a licence for two years.'

'Go and fetch the blue Peugeot and wait for me downstairs. Make sure there's petrol in it.' And to Janvier, who was looking disappointed: 'Take another car and drive there slowly, questioning garage owners, innkeepers, whoever you like. It's possible someone else noticed the brown car. I'll see you in Lagny.'

He had another glass of beer. A few minutes later, Dr Paul appeared, with his merry beard, and got into the car that Lapointe was proudly driving.

'Shall I take the shortest route?'

'Preferably, young man.'

It was one of the first fine days and there were a lot of cars on the road, filled with families.

Dr Paul told anecdotes about post-mortems, which, in his mouth, became as funny as Jewish jokes or tall tales.

In Lagny, they had to ask for directions, leave the town itself and make a long detour before they came to a bend in the river where a crane stood, surrounded by at least a hundred people. The gendarmes were having as much difficulty controlling the crowds as if the fair was on. The lieutenant of gendarmes seemed relieved when he recognized Maigret.

There, lying across the embankment, was the chocolate-brown car, covered in mud, grass and all kinds of unidentifiable detritus, water still gushing from every crevice. The bodywork was twisted, one of the windows was broken and the two headlights were shattered, but, remarkably, one door was still in working order, and it was through this that the body had been removed.

The body itself formed a little heap under a tarpaulin, and those bystanders who approached it found themselves retching.

'I'll let you work, doctor.'

'Here?'

Dr Paul would have been happy to do so. He had been known to do post-mortems in the unlikeliest places, an inevitable cigarette in his mouth, even stopping and taking off his rubber gloves to have a bite to eat.

'Can you take the body to the gendarmerie, lieutenant?'

'My men will deal with it. Get back, you others. And the children! Who's letting children come so close?'

Maigret was examining the car when an old woman pulled him by the sleeve and said proudly, 'It was me who found her.'

'Are you the widow Hébart?'

'Hubart, monsieur. The house over there behind the ash trees is mine.'

'Tell me what you saw.'

'Strictly speaking, I didn't see anything, but I heard. I was coming back along the towpath. That's where we are now.'

'Had you been drinking a lot?'

'Just two or three little glasses.'

'Where were you?'

'Fifty metres further on, nearer to my house. I heard a car coming from the main road. I thought it must have been poachers again. Because it was too cold for lovers, and it was raining. When I turned round, all I saw was the headlights.

'How was I supposed to know it was going to be important one day? I carried on walking, and I had the impression the car had stopped.'

'Because you couldn't hear the engine any more?'

'That's right.'

'You had your back to the path?'

'Yes. Then I heard the engine again, and I thought the car was making a U-turn. But it didn't! Immediately afterwards, there was a big splash, and when I turned round, the car wasn't there any more.'

'You didn't hear anybody screaming?'

'No.'

'You didn't retrace your steps?'

'Should I have? What could I have done all by myself? It had upset me. I thought the poor people must have drowned, and I rushed home to have a stiff drink to recover.'

'You didn't stay on the riverbank?'

'No, monsieur.'

'And you didn't hear anything else after the splash?'

'I thought I heard something like footsteps, but I thought it was a rabbit that had been startled by the noise.'

'Is that all?'

'Don't you think that's enough? If they'd listened to me instead of calling me a mad old woman, that lady would have been out of the water a long time ago. Did you see her?'

Not without a grimace of disgust, Maigret imagined this old woman contemplating the other old woman in her decomposed state.

Did the widow Hubart realize that she was only alive by a miracle, and that, if she had been curious enough to turn back that famous night, she might well have followed the other woman into the Marne?

'Will there be reporters here?'

It was the reporters she was waiting for, because she wanted to have her picture in the papers.

Lapointe emerged, covered in mud, from the Chrysler, which he had been examining. 'I didn't find anything,' he said. 'The tools are in their place in the boot, with the spare tyre. There's no luggage, not even a handbag. There was only a woman's shoe jammed in the bottom of the seat and, in the dashboard box, this pair of gloves and this torch.'

The gloves were pigskin – men's gloves, as far as it was still possible to judge.

'Go to the railway station. Someone must have taken the train that evening. Unless there are taxis in the town. Join me at the gendarmerie.'

He preferred to wait in the courtyard, smoking his pipe, until Dr Paul, who had been installed in the garage, had finished his work.

8. The Family with the Toys

'Are you disappointed, sir?'

Young Lapointe really would have liked to call him 'chief', like Lucas, Torrence, and most of those in the team, but he felt too new for that. It seemed to him a privilege he had to acquire, like earning your stripes.

They had just driven Dr Paul home and were on their way back to the Quai des Orfèvres. Paris seemed even more filled with light after the hours spent wading in the darkness of Lagny. From the Pont Saint-Michel, Maigret could see lights in his own office.

'No, I'm not disappointed. I wasn't expecting the staff at the station to remember travellers whose tickets they punched a month ago.'

'I was wondering what you were thinking about?'

He replied quite naturally, 'The suitcase.'

'I swear to you it was in the workshop when I went to the bookbinder's that first time.'

'I don't doubt that.'

'And I'm certain it wasn't the suitcase Sergeant Lucas found in the basement in the afternoon.'

'I don't doubt that either. Leave the car in the courtyard and come upstairs.'

It was clear from how animated the few men on duty were

that there was news, and as soon as Lucas heard Maigret come in he threw open the door of his office.

'Information about Moss, chief. A young girl and her father came here earlier. They wanted to speak to you personally, but after waiting nearly two hours they finally made up their minds to give me the message. The girl's about sixteen or seventeen, very pretty, very round and pink, and looks people straight in the eyes. The father's a sculptor who once, if I understood correctly, won the Prix de Rome. There's another girl, who's a bit older, and a mother. They live on Boulevard Pasteur, where they make toys. Unless I'm mistaken, the girl came with her father to stop him drinking on the way, it seems to be his little weakness. He wears a big black hat and a floppy tie. Moss has been staying in their apartment for the past few months, under the name Peeters.'

'Is he still there?'

'If he were, I'd already have sent some inspectors to arrest him, or rather, I'd have gone there myself. He left them on March 12th.'

'In other words, the day Levine, Gloria and the child vanished into thin air after the scene in Square d'Anvers.'

'He didn't tell them he was leaving. He went out in the morning as usual, and hasn't set foot in the apartment since. I thought you'd prefer to question them yourself. Oh, another thing. Philippe Liotard has already phoned twice.'

'What did he want?'

'To speak to you. If you came back before eleven tonight, he wanted you to call him at the Chope du Nègre.'

A brasserie Maigret knew, on Boulevard Bonne-Nouvelle.

'Give me the Chope!'

It was the cashier who answered. She had Liotard fetched to the phone.

'Is that you, inspector? I suppose you must be snowed under with work. Did you find him?'

'Who?'

'Moss. I went to the cinema this afternoon, and I understood. Don't you think a man-to-man talk, strictly off the record, might be useful to both of us?'

It happened by chance. A little earlier, in the car, Maigret had been thinking about the suitcase. Now, just as Liotard was speaking to him, young Lapointe came into the office.

'Are you with friends?' Maigret asked Liotard.

'It doesn't matter. When you get here, I won't sit with them any more.'

'Your girlfriend?'

'Yes.'

'Anybody else?'

'Someone you don't like very much, I don't know why. He's very upset about it.'

In other words, Alfonsi. There must be four of them again, the two men and their girlfriends.

'I'll be there, but I might be late. Will you wait for me?'

'I'll wait as long as you like. It's Sunday.'

'Tell Alfonsi I'd like to see him too.'

'He'll be delighted.'

'See you later, then.'

Maigret motioned to Lapointe, who had been discreetly

trying to leave, that he should stay, and then went and closed both doors of his office.

'Come here. Sit down. You really want to do well in the police, don't you?'

'It matters more to me than anything else.'

'You were stupid enough to talk too much on the first day, and you still have no idea what that's led to.'

'I'm really sorry. I genuinely trusted my sister.'

'Would you like to do something difficult for me? Hold on, don't answer too quickly. I'm not talking about something spectacular that'll get your name in the papers. On the contrary. If you succeed, only the two of us will know about it. If you fail, I'll be forced to disown you and say you were over-zealous and did something I hadn't told you to do.'

'I understand.'

'You don't understand at all, but that doesn't matter. If I did this thing myself and failed, the whole police force would be implicated. But that won't happen to you, you're too new to the organization.'

Lapointe could hardly contain his impatience.

'Maître Liotard and Alfonsi are at the Chope du Nègre right now, waiting for me.'

'Are you going to join them?'

'Not straight away. I want to go to Boulevard Pasteur first, and I'm sure they won't leave the Chope before I get there. Let's say I join them in an hour at the earliest. It's nine o'clock now. You know Liotard's apartment in Rue Bergère? It's on the third floor, on the left. As a good few ladies of easy virtue live in the building, the concierge probably doesn't pay too much attention to people coming and going.'

'You want me to . . .'

'Yes. You've been taught how to open a door. It won't matter too much if you leave any signs of entry. On the contrary. And there's no point searching the drawers, or looking through papers. You just have to check one thing: that the suitcase isn't there.'

'I hadn't thought of that.'

'Well, it's possible, even likely, that it isn't there, because Liotard's a cautious fellow. That's why you mustn't waste any time. From Rue Bergère, go to Rue de Douai, where Alfonsi has Room 33 in the Hôtel du Massif Central.'

'I know it.'

'Do the same thing there. The suitcase. Nothing else. Phone me as soon as you've finished.'

'Can I go now?'

'Go out into the corridor first. I'm going to lock my door and I want you to try and open it. Ask Lucas for the tools.'

Lapointe didn't do too badly, and a few minutes later he rushed out, overjoyed.

Maigret went into the inspectors' room. 'Are you free, Janvier?'

The telephones were still ringing, but less frantically, because of the hour.

'I was helping Lucas, but . . .'

They both went downstairs, and it was Janvier who got in behind the wheel of the police car. A quarter of an hour later, they reached the quietest, most dimly lit part of Boulevard Pasteur, which, in the peace of a beautiful Sunday evening, could have been an avenue in a small town.

'Come up with me.'

They asked for the sculptor, whose name was Grossot, and were directed to the sixth floor. The building was old, but very decent: it was probably inhabited by minor civil servants. When they knocked at the door on the sixth floor, sounds of an argument came to an abrupt halt, and a round-cheeked young girl opened then stood aside.

'Was it you who came to my office earlier?'

'That was my sister. Are you Detective Chief Inspector Maigret? Come in. Don't mind the mess. We were just finishing dinner.'

She led them into a very large studio with a sloping ceiling, part of it of glass, through which the stars could be seen. On a long white wooden table were what remained of a dish of cold meats and a started litre bottle of wine. Another young girl, who looked like the twin of the one who had opened the door, was arranging her hair with a furtive gesture, while a man in a velvet jacket advanced towards the visitors with exaggerated solemnity.

'Welcome to my modest abode, Monsieur Maigret. I hope you'll do me the honour of having a drink with me.'

Since he had left the Quai des Orfèvres, the old sculptor must have found a way to drink something else apart from the wine he'd had with his meal, because his speech was slurred and his walk unsteady.

'Don't take any notice,' one of the girls broke in. 'He's got himself in a state again.'

She said this without any bitterness in her voice, throwing her father an affectionate, almost maternal look.

In the darkest corners of the large room, sculptures could be made out, and it was clear they had been there for a long time.

More recent, part of their present life, were the wooden toys cluttering the furniture and spreading a nice smell of fresh wood through the room.

'When art is no longer enough to support a man and his family,' Grossot declaimed, 'there's no shame in turning to commerce for one's daily bread, is there?'

Madame Grossot appeared now: she had probably gone to tidy herself up when she heard knocking at the door. She was a thin, sad-looking woman, her eyes constantly on the alert, who must always be expecting misfortune.

'Aren't you going to give these gentlemen chairs, Hélène?'

'The inspector knows perfectly well he can make himself at home, Mother. Isn't that right, Monsieur Maigret?'

'Haven't you offered him anything?'

'Would you like a glass of wine? There's nothing else in the house, because of Daddy.'

It was she who seemed to be in charge of the family, she in any case who took over the conversation.

'We went to the local cinema last night, and we recognized the man you're looking for. He didn't call himself Moss, but Peeters. The only reason we didn't come to see you earlier was that Daddy was reluctant to betray him, objecting that he was our guest and had often eaten at our table.'

'Had he been living here long?'

'About a year. The apartment covers the whole floor. My parents have been living here for more than thirty years and I was born here, as was my sister. Apart from the studio and the kitchen, there are three bedrooms. Last year, because of the financial crisis, we didn't earn much from the toys, so we decided to take a lodger. We put an ad in the newspaper.

'That's how we met Monsieur Peeters.'

'What did he say his profession was?'

'He told us he represented a big English company, and that he had his regular customers, which meant that he didn't need to travel around much. He sometimes spent all day here. He'd come and give us a hand in his shirt-sleeves. We all work on the toys together, after my father makes the models. Last Christmas, we got an order from Printemps, and we worked round the clock.'

Grossot was squinting so pitifully at the half-empty litre bottle that Maigret said, 'Go on, then, I'll join you in a drink. Pour me half a glass.'

In return, he received a look of gratitude.

'He usually went out late in the afternoon and sometimes came back quite late at night,' the girl continued, her eyes on her father to make sure he didn't pour himself too large a glass. 'Sometimes he took his sample case with him.'

'Did he leave his luggage here?'

'He left his big trunk.'

'Not his suitcase?'

'No. Actually, Olga, did he have his suitcase with him when he left?'

'No. He didn't bring it back with him the last time he went out with it.'

'What kind of man was he?'

'He was quiet, mild-mannered, maybe a little sad. Sometimes he'd shut himself up in his room for hours and we'd end up going and asking him if he was ill. At other times, he had breakfast with us and helped us all day.

'He was sometimes away for several days, but he always warned us in advance.'

'What did you call him?'

'Monsieur Jean. He'd call us by our first names, except my mother, of course. He sometimes brought us chocolates or little gifts.'

'Never anything valuable?'

'We wouldn't have accepted it.'

'Did he have visitors?'

'No, nobody ever came to see him. He didn't get any mail either. I was surprised that a travelling salesman shouldn't receive any letters, but he told me he had an associate in town, with an office, and that was where his correspondence was sent.'

'Did he ever strike you as strange?'

She looked around her and said, without insisting, 'In a place like this?'

'Your health, Monsieur Maigret. To your investigation! As you can see, I'm nobody these days, not only in the field of art, but in my own home. I don't protest. I don't say anything. They're nice girls, but, for a man who—'

'Let him speak, Daddy.'

'You see what I mean?'

'Do you know when your lodger last went out with his suitcase?'

It was Olga, the elder daughter, who replied, 'The last Saturday before . . .'

She hesitated, unsure whether she should continue.

'Before what?'

The younger girl resumed control of the conversation. 'Don't blush, Olga. We were always teasing my sister, who had a bit of a crush on Monsieur Jean. He was too old for her, and he wasn't handsome, but . . .'

'What about you?'

'Never mind that. One Saturday, about six o'clock, he left with his suitcase, which surprised us, because it was usually Monday when he took it with him.'

'Monday afternoon?'

'Yes. We didn't expect him back, thinking he'd be spending the weekend somewhere, and we teased Olga because she had such a long face.'

'That's not true.'

'What time he came back, we don't know. Usually, we heard him open the door. On Sunday morning, we thought the apartment was empty and we were just talking about him when he came out of his room, looking ill, and asked my father to go and get him a bottle of brandy. He claimed he'd caught a cold. He stayed in bed part of the day. When Olga did his room, she noticed that the suitcase wasn't there. She noticed something else, at any rate she claims she did.'

'I'm sure of it.'

'It's possible. You always looked at him more closely than we did.'

'I'm sure his suit wasn't the same. It was a blue suit, like the other one, but not his, and when he put it on I noticed it was a bit too wide in the shoulders.'

'Did he say anything about it?'

'No. We didn't mention it either. That was when he complained that he had the flu and didn't go out for a whole week.'

'Did he read the newspapers?'

'The morning paper and the evening paper, just like us.'

'You didn't notice anything else unusual?'

'No. Except that he went and locked himself in his room as soon as anybody knocked at the door.'

'When did he start going out again?'

'About a week later. The last time he slept here was the night of March 11th. I'm sure of that because of the calendar in his room. The pages haven't been torn off since then.'

'What should we do, inspector?' the mother asked anxiously. 'Do you really think he committed a crime?'

'I don't know, madame.'

'But if the police are looking for him . . .'

'Do you mind if we have a look at his room?'

It was at the end of a corridor. Spacious, not luxurious, but clean, with old polished furniture, and reproductions of Michelangelo on the walls. A huge black trunk, of the most common kind, stood in the right-hand corner, with a rope around it.

'Will you open it, Janvier?'

'Should I leave the room?' the girl asked.

He didn't see the need. Janvier had more difficulty with the rope than with the lock, which was an ordinary one. A strong smell of mothballs invaded the room. They started piling suits, shoes and underwear on the bed.

It was like an actor's wardrobe, so varied were the clothes in quality and origin. A suit and a dinner-jacket both bore labels from a major London tailor, and another suit had been made in Milan.

There were also white linen suits of the kind worn mainly in hot countries, some quite garish suits, and others, on the contrary, which wouldn't have looked out of place on a bank teller. For all of them, they found matching shoes, made in Paris, Nice, Brussels, Rotterdam and Berlin.

Finally, right at the bottom, separated from the rest by a sheet of brown paper, they dug up a clown's costume, which surprised the girl even more than all the rest.

'Is he an actor?'

'A kind of actor.'

There was nothing else revealing in the room. The blue suit they had been talking about wasn't there, because Peeters-Moss had been wearing it when he left. Perhaps he was still wearing it.

In the drawers, there were all kinds of objects – cigarette cases, wallets, buttons for sleeves and false collars, keys, a broken pipe – but not a single paper, and no address book either.

'I'm very grateful, mademoiselle. You did well to inform us, and I'm convinced you'll have no problems. I don't suppose you have a telephone?'

'We had one several years ago, but . . .' And then, in a low voice: 'Daddy wasn't always like this. That's why we can't be angry with him. He never used to drink at all. Then he met some friends from the Beaux-Arts who are all more or less in the same boat as him, and he started getting together with them in a little café in Saint-Germain. It doesn't do them any good.'

On a workbench in the studio there were a number of precision machines for sawing, filing and planing the sometimes tiny pieces of wood from which they made elegant toys.

'Put a little sawdust in a piece of paper, Janvier. We'll take it with us.'

That would please Moers. It was amusing to think that Moers' tests would probably have led them here anyway, to this apartment perched high in a building on Boulevard Pasteur. It would have taken weeks, perhaps months, but they would have got here in the end.

It was ten o'clock. The bottle of wine was empty and Grossot suggested going downstairs with 'these gentlemen', but wasn't allowed.

'I'll probably be back.'

'What about him?'

'I'd be surprised. In any case, I don't think you have anything to fear from him.'

'Where can I take you, chief?' Janvier asked as they got back in the car.

'Boulevard Bonne-Nouvelle. Drop me a little distance from the Chope du Nègre and wait for me.'

It was one of those big brasseries that served choucroute and sausages and where, on Saturday and Sunday evenings, four scrawny musicians played on a little stage. Maigret immediately spotted the two couples, sitting at a table near the window, and noticed that the women had ordered crème de menthes.

Alfonsi was the first to stand, not all that confidently, like a man who expects a kick up his backside, while Liotard smiled and held out his well-groomed hand, very much in control.

'May I introduce our lady friends?'

He did so, condescendingly.

'Will you sit with us for a moment, or would you prefer to move to another table immediately?'

'Provided Alfonsi keeps these ladies company and waits for me, I prefer to talk to you in private for the moment.'

A table was free near the cash register. Most of the customers were local shopkeepers, treating themselves to a family meal out, as Maigret had done the evening before. There were also the regular customers, bachelors or unhappily married men playing cards or chess.

'What will you have? A beer? A beer and a fine à l'eau, waiter.'

Soon, Liotard would probably be frequenting the bars of the Opéra and the Champs-Élysées, but for now he still felt more at home in this neighbourhood, where he could look at people with a grand air of superiority.

'Did your appeal yield any results?'

'Did you ask for me to come and see you so that you could question me, Maître Liotard?'

'To make peace, perhaps. How would you feel about that? It's possible I've been a bit abrupt with you. Don't forget we're on different sides. Your job is to condemn my client, mine to save him.'

'By becoming his accomplice?'

The blow hit home. Liotard blinked two or three times and pinched his long nostrils. 'I don't know what you mean. But since that's the way you like it, I'll get straight to the point. The thing is, detective chief inspector, you're in a position to do me a great deal of harm. You could slow down a career that everyone agrees might well turn out brilliant. You could even put a stop to it altogether.'

'I don't doubt that.'

'Thank you. The Bar Council is quite strict about certain rules, and I admit that, in my haste to get on, I haven't always followed them.'

Maigret was drinking his beer with the most innocent air in the world, all the while watching the cashier, who probably thought he was the local hatter.

'I'm waiting, Monsieur Liotard.'

'I was hoping you'd help me, because you know perfectly well what I'm referring to.'

Maigret still did not react.

'You see, detective chief inspector, I belong to a very poor family . . ."

'The Comtes de Liotard?'

'I said very poor, not common. I had a lot of difficulty paying for my studies and I was forced to do all kinds of jobs when I was a student. I was even a uniformed usher in a cinema on the Grands Boulevards.'

'Good for you.'

'Even a month ago, I wasn't eating every day. Like all my colleagues of my age, and even some who are older, I was waiting for a case that would get me noticed.'

'You found it.'

'I found it. That's what I'm getting at. On Friday, in Judge Dossin's office, you said certain things that made me think you knew a lot and that you wouldn't hesitate to use it against me.'

'Against you?'

'Against my client, if you prefer.'

'I don't understand.'

Maigret ordered another beer: he had seldom drunk such good beer, especially as it made a nice contrast with the sculptor's warm wine. He was still looking at the cashier, as if delighted that she was so much like the cashiers he'd seen in cafés in the old days, with her powerful chest lifted by her corset, her black silk blouse adorned with a cameo, her hair swept up into the shape of a wedding cake.

'You were saying?'

'I see you're determined to make me talk. Well, you're absolutely right: I committed a professional error by offering my services to Frans Steuvels.'

'Only one?'

'I found out about the case in the most banal way possible, and I hope nobody will get into trouble because of me. I'm quite good friends with a man named Antoine Bizard, we live in the same building. We've both had difficulty making ends meet, and we've sometimes shared a tin of sardines or a camembert. Lately, Bizard has had a regular job on a newspaper. He has a girlfriend.'

'The sister of one of my inspectors.'

'You see? You know.'

'I'd like to hear you say it.'

'Through his work on the newspaper, where he does the fillers, Bizard is in a position to know about certain things before the public.'

'Crimes, for example.'

'For example. He's got into the habit of phoning me.'

'So that you can then go and offer your services?'

'You're a cruel victor, Monsieur Maigret.'

'Carry on.'

He was still watching the cashier, while also checking that Alfonsi was keeping the two women company.

'I was informed that the police were taking an interest in a bookbinder in Rue de Turenne.'

'On February 21st, early in the afternoon.'

'That's correct. I went over there and really did talk about an ex-libris before bringing up a more burning subject.'

'The stove.'

'That's all. I told Steuvels that, if he was in any trouble, I'd be happy to defend him. All that, you know. It wasn't so much for me that I wanted to have this conversation with you tonight – and I hope it remains strictly confidential – it was more for my client. Anything that harmed me right now would harm him indirectly. There you are, Monsieur Maigret. It's for you to decide. Tomorrow morning, I could be disbarred. You just have to see the president of the bar and tell him what you know.'

'How long were you at the bookbinder's?'

'A quarter of an hour at the most.'

'Did you see his wife?'

'I think at one point she stuck her head out above the stairs.'

'Did Steuvels tell you anything in confidence?'

'No. I'm ready to give you my word.'

'One more question, maître. Since when has Alfonsi been working for you?'

'He doesn't work for me. He has a private detective agency.'

'With himself as the only employee!'

'That's none of my business. To defend my client with any chance of success, I need certain information I can't exactly gather myself.'

'Above all, you needed to find out how much I knew day by day.'

'All's fair in love and war, isn't it?'

At the cash desk, the telephone rang. The cashier picked up the receiver.

'Just a moment. I don't know. I'll check.'

As she was opening her mouth to give the waiter a name, Maigret stood up. 'Is it for me?'

'What's your name?'

'Maigret.'

'Do you want me to put it through to the booth?'

'There's no need, it'll only take a few seconds.' It was the call he'd been expecting from Lapointe. The young man's voice was shaking with emotion.

'Is that you, sir? I have it!'

'Where?'

'I didn't find anything at the lawyer's, where I was almost caught by the concierge. As you told me to, I then went to Rue de Douai. Everybody goes in and out there, so it was easy. I had no difficulty opening the door. The suitcase was under the bed. What should I do?'

'Where are you?'

'At the tobacconist's on the corner of Rue de Douai.'

'Take a taxi back to the Quai. I'll see you there.'

'OK, chief. Are you pleased?' Carried away by his enthusiasm and pride, he had allowed himself, for the first time, to use the word 'chief'. But he still needed reassurance.

'You did a good job.'

Liotard was watching Maigret anxiously. Maigret resumed his seat on the banquette with a satisfied sigh, and signalled to the waiter.

'Another beer. And maybe you could bring a fine for monsieur.'

'But—'

'Don't worry, son.'

That word was enough to alert Liotard.

'You see, it's not the Bar Council I'm going to talk to about you. It's the public prosecutor. Tomorrow morning, it's quite likely I'll ask him for two arrest warrants, one in your name, and one for your associate Alfonsi.'

'Are you joking?'

'What will you get for that, a conviction for receiving stolen goods in a murder case? I'll have to check in the penal code. I need to think about it. Can I leave you to settle the bill?'

Already standing, he leaned over Philippe Liotard's shoulder and added softly, confidentially:

'I have the suitcase!'

9. *The Dieppe Photograph*

Maigret had already called the judge's office once, about half past nine, and spoken to the clerk.

'Could you ask Judge Dossin if he can see me?'

'He's right here.'

'Anything new?' the judge had asked. 'I mean apart from what the press is saying this morning?'

He was in a very excited state. The morning papers carried the news of the discovery of the chocolate-brown car and the body of the old woman in Lagny.

'I think so. I'm coming to tell you about it.'

But since then, whenever Maigret had headed for the door of his office, something had delayed him: a phone call, the arrival of an inspector with something to report. Discreetly, the judge had called back and asked Lucas, 'Is the detective chief inspector still there?'

'Yes. Shall I put you through to him?

'No. I suppose he's busy. I'm sure he'll come upstairs in a while.'

At a quarter past ten, he had finally made up his mind to call Maigret.

'Sorry to bother you. I imagine you're snowed under. But I've summoned Frans Steuvels for eleven o'clock, and

I wouldn't like to start the interrogation without seeing you first.'

'Would it bother you if I brought someone else in?'

'Who?'

'His wife, probably. If you don't mind, I'll have her fetched by an inspector just in case.'

'Do you want an official summons?'

'That won't be necessary.'

Judge Dossin waited another ten minutes, intending to study the file. At last, there was a knock at his door. He almost rushed to it and saw Maigret standing there with a suitcase in his hand.

'Are you going away?'

Maigret's smile informed him otherwise, and he murmured, unable to believe his eyes, 'Is that the suitcase?'

'It's heavy, I can tell you that.'

'So we were right?'

He was relieved of a great weight. Philippe Liotard's systematic campaign had worn him down in the end. After all, it was he who had taken responsibility for keeping Steuvels in prison.

'Is he guilty?'

'Guilty enough to be put inside for a few years.'

Maigret had known the contents of the suitcase since the previous evening, but he went through them again, with the same pleasure as a child laying out his Christmas gifts.

What weighed down this brown suitcase, its handle repaired with string, were pieces of metal that looked rather like a bookbinder's stamps, but were actually the seals of various countries.

In particular there was a seal from the United States, and seals from all the countries of South America.

There were also rubber stamps such as those used in town halls and government offices, all laid out as neatly as a salesman's samples.

'This is Steuvels' work,' Maigret explained. 'His brother Alfred provided him with the moulds and the blank passports. As far as I've been able to judge from these examples, the passports aren't forgeries, they've actually been stolen from consulates.'

'Had they been doing this for a long time?'

'I don't think so. Roughly two years, according to the bank accounts. This morning, I put calls through to most of the banks in Paris. That's partly what stopped me coming up to see you earlier.'

'Steuvels has his account in the Société Générale in Rue Saint-Antoine, doesn't he?'

'He has another account in an American bank on Place Vendôme, and another still in an English bank on the boulevard. So far, we've found five different accounts. It started two years ago, which corresponds with the time his brother came back to Paris.'

It was raining. The weather was grey and mild. Maigret was sitting by the window, smoking his pipe.

'You see, your honour, Alfred Moss isn't a professional villain. Professionals have a speciality which they keep to most of the time. I've never seen a pickpocket taking up burglary, or a burglar passing false cheques or becoming a con man.

'Alfred Moss was a clown to start with, an acrobat.

'It was after a fall that he became a criminal. Unless I'm very much mistaken, he did his first job by chance. Thanks to his knowledge of languages, he'd been hired as an interpreter in a big hotel in London. The opportunity presented itself to steal some jewellery and he did so.

'He lived off that for a while. Not for very long, because he has a vice, something else I only found out about this morning, thanks to the manager of the local betting shop: he plays the horses.

'Like any amateur, he didn't keep to one kind of theft, he tried everything.

'He was unusually skilful. Lucky too, because he was never convicted.

'He had his highs and lows. One day he passed a false cheque, the next he played a con trick.

'As he got older, he saw himself discredited in most capital cities, blacklisted from the big hotels where he used to operate.'

'Is that when he remembered his brother?'

'Yes. Two years ago, gold smuggling, which was his previous activity, stopped bringing in much income. False passports, on the other hand, especially for America, were starting to reach astronomic sums. He told himself that a bookbinder, accustomed to making coats of arms with blocking stamps, would probably make a decent job of official seals.'

'What surprises me is that Steuvels agreed to it. He doesn't need the money. Unless he has a double life we haven't discovered.'

'He doesn't have a double life. Poverty, real poverty, the kind he knew in his childhood and adolescence, produces two kinds of people: spendthrifts and misers. Mostly misers, who are so afraid of the bad old days coming back that they're capable of anything to ensure against them.

'If I'm not mistaken, that's the case with Steuvels. The list of banks where he's made deposits is evidence of that. I'm convinced it wasn't a way of hiding his assets, because it never even occurred to him that he might be found out. But he was suspicious of banks, nationalizations, devaluations, so he put small sums in different establishments.'

'I thought he practically never left his wife.'

'That's correct. She was the one who left him. It took me a while to discover it. Every Monday afternoon, she's been going to the Vert-Galant laundry boat to do her washing. Almost every Monday, Moss arrived with his suitcase, and whenever he was early he'd wait in the Tabac des Vosges for his sister-in-law to leave.

'The two brothers had the afternoon to themselves to work. The tools and the passports never stayed in Rue de Turenne. Moss would take them away with him.

'Some Mondays, Steuvels still had time to rush to one of his banks and make a deposit.'

'I don't see where the young woman with the boy comes in, or the countess, or—'

'I'm coming to that, your honour. The reason I've talked first about the suitcase is because that's what bothered me most, right from the start. But since I heard about Moss and suspected what he was up to, another question has been uppermost in my thoughts.

'Why, when the gang had been keeping their heads down, was there a sudden stir on Tuesday, March 12th, which ended with them all scattering?

'I'm talking about the incident in Square d'Anvers, which my wife just happened to witness.

'The previous day, Moss was still living quietly in his room on Boulevard Pasteur.

'Levine and the child were staying at the Hôtel Beauséjour, where Gloria came every day to take the child out for a walk.

'But that Tuesday, at about ten in the morning, Moss goes to the Hôtel Beauséjour where, presumably as a precaution, he's never before set foot.

'Levine immediately packs his bags, rushes to Place d'Anvers and attracts the attention of Gloria, who leaves the child high and dry and follows him.

'By the afternoon, they've all vanished without a trace.

'So what happened on the morning of March 12th?

'Moss didn't receive a phone call, because there's no telephone in the apartment where he was living.

'At that point, my inspectors and I hadn't done anything that might have frightened the gang. We didn't know about them.

'As for Frans Steuvels, he was in the Santé.

'But something did happen.

'It was only last night, when I got home, that quite by chance I found the answer to that question.'

Judge Dossin was so relieved to know that the man he had put in prison was not innocent that he smiled ecstatically as he listened to Maigret, as if listening to a fascinating story.

'My wife spent the evening waiting for me and took advantage of it to do something she's been doing for a while now. Every now and again, she puts press cuttings about me into exercise books. She's been particularly keen on doing that since a former director of the Police Judiciaire published his memoirs.

'When I tease her about it, she always says, "You may well write yours one day, when you retire and we're living in the country."

'Anyway, when I got back last night, the pot of glue and the scissors were on the table. As I took my things off, I happened to glance over my wife's shoulder, and in one of the cuttings she was about to put in, I saw a photograph I'd forgotten.

'It was taken three years ago, by a young reporter in Normandy: my wife and I were spending a few days in Dieppe, and he caught us in the doorway of our boarding house.

'What surprised me was seeing that photograph on a page from a magazine.

'"Haven't you read it? It appeared quite recently: a four-page article about your early years and your methods."

'There were other photographs, including one where I was a secretary in a local police station and had a long moustache.

'"When does it date from?"

'"The article? Last week. I didn't have time to show it to you. You're almost never at home these days."

'To cut a long story short, the article appeared in a Parisian weekly which went on sale on the morning of Tuesday, March 12th.

'I immediately sent someone to the people who were still putting up Moss at that date, and got confirmation that the younger of the girls had brought up the magazine at about 8.30, at the same time as the milk, and that Moss had glanced at it while having his breakfast.

'From that point on, everything becomes simple. It even explains why Gloria spent so much time on that bench in Square d'Anvers.

'After those two murders and the arrest of Steuvels, the gang had scattered and were in hiding. Levine probably changed hotels several times before ending up in Rue Lepic. As a precaution, he was never seen outside with Gloria, and they even avoided sleeping in the same place.

'Every morning, Moss had to go to Square d'Anvers to get news. All he had to do was sit on the end of the bench.

'Now as you know, my wife sat on the same bench three or four times while waiting to see the dentist. The two women had made each other's acquaintance and got chatting. Moss had probably seen Madame Maigret, but hadn't paid any attention to her.

'Imagine his reaction on discovering, through the magazine, that the good lady on the bench was none other than the wife of the inspector in charge of the investigation!

'He couldn't imagine it was coincidence, could he? He quite naturally assumed we were on his trail and that I'd given my wife a role in the investigation.

'He rushed to Rue Lepic and alerted Levine, who then ran to warn Gloria.'

'Why did they argue?'

'Maybe because of the boy. Maybe Levine didn't want Gloria to go back for him and run the risk of being arrested. She insisted she wanted to go back, but that she'd take as many precautions as possible.

'Which inclines me to think, by the way, that they won't be together when we eventually track them down. They probably think we know about Gloria and the boy, but don't know anything about Levine. He and Moss must have gone their separate ways.'

'Do you think you'll ever get your hands on them?'

'Maybe tomorrow, maybe in a year. You know how these things are.'

'You still haven't told me where you discovered the suit-case.'

'You might prefer not to know how we came into its possession. The fact is, I was forced to use a not very legal method, for which I take full responsibility, but of which you may not approve.

'All you need to know is that it was Liotard who relieved Steuvels of the compromising suitcase.

'For one reason or another, Moss took the suitcase to Rue de Turenne that Saturday night and left it there.

'Frans Steuvels simply pushed it under a table in his workshop, thinking nobody would notice it.

'On February 21st, Lapointe showed up under a pretext and visited the premises.

'Don't forget, Steuvels couldn't reach his brother, or anybody in the gang I imagine, to bring them up to date. I think I know what happened next.

'He must have been wondering how to get rid of the

suitcase, probably waiting for it to get dark before he dealt with it, when Liotard, whom he'd never heard of, showed up.'

'How did Liotard find out?'

'Through an indiscretion in my department.'

'One of your inspectors?'

'I don't blame him for it, and it's unlikely to happen again. Anyway, Liotard offered his services, more services in fact than might be expected from a member of the bar, since he took the suitcase away.'

'So it was in his place that you found it?'

'No, he'd passed it to Alfonsi.'

'So to sum up, where are we now?'

'Nowhere. I mean we still don't know anything about the most important thing, in other words, the two murders. A man was killed in Rue de Turenne, and before that, the Countess Panetti was killed in her car, we don't know where. You must have received Dr Paul's report by now. There was a bullet in the old woman's skull.

'But I have just had a bit of information from Italy. More than a year ago, the Krynkers got divorced in Switzerland, because there's no divorce in Italy. The Countess Panetti's daughter got married again, to an American, and the two of them are now living in Texas.'

'She didn't reconcile with her mother?'

'On the contrary. Her mother was more upset than ever. Krynker is Hungarian, from a good family, but poor. He spent part of the winter in Monte Carlo, trying, without success, to make a fortune from gambling.

'He arrived in Paris three weeks before the death of his

former mother-in-law and stayed first at the Commodore, then in a little hotel in Rue Caumartin.'

'How long had Gloria Lotti been working for the old lady?'

'Four or five months. We're not entirely sure yet.'

They heard noises in the corridor, and the usher came to announce that Steuvels had arrived.

'Shall I tell him all this?' Judge Dossin asked, once again embarrassed by his responsibilities.

'Two things may happen. Either he'll talk, or he'll continue to keep quiet. I've had to deal with a few Flemish people in my time, and I've learned that they keep things close to their chests. If he keeps quiet, things may drag on for weeks or even longer. We may not find out anything until we track down one of the four people who've gone to earth somewhere or other.'

'Four?'

'Moss, Levine, the woman and the boy. We may have most chance of finding the boy.'

'Unless they've got rid of him.'

'The fact that Gloria went to collect him from my wife suggests he means a lot to her.'

'Do you think he's her son?'

'I'm convinced he is. The mistake is to believe that criminals aren't people like anyone else, people who might have children and love them.'

'Is Levine the father?'

'Probably.'

As Dossin stood up, he gave a weak smile that was not lacking in either mischief or humility. 'I think this might be time for the third degree, don't you? Unfortunately, I'm not very good at that kind of thing.'

'If you'll allow me, I can try having a word with Liotard.'

'To get him to advise his client to talk?'

'Given where we are now, it's in both their interests.'

'So I shouldn't ask them in immediately?'

'Just wait a bit.'

Maigret went out. To the man seated to the right of the door, on a bench worn smooth by use, he said cordially, 'Good morning, Steuvels.'

Just then, Janvier appeared in the corridor, accompanied by Fernande, who looked quite emotional. For a moment, Maigret hesitated over whether or not to let her join her husband. But then he said to both of them, 'You have time for a chat. The judge isn't quite ready yet.'

He motioned to Liotard to follow him, and they spoke in low voices, walking up and down the grey corridor, where there were gendarmes in front of most of the doors. The discussion lasted barely five minutes.

'When you're ready, just knock.'

Maigret went back into the judge's office alone, leaving Liotard, Steuvels and Fernande in conversation.

'What happened?'

'We're going to find out. Liotard is happy to go along with it, obviously. I can cook up a nice little report for you in which I talk about the suitcase without bringing him into it.'

'That's not very legal, is it?'

'Do you want to get your hands on the murderers?'

'I understand you, Maigret. But my father and grandfather were both on the bench, and I think that's where I'm going to end up too.'

His face was red as he waited with a mixture of impatience and fear for a knock at the door.

The door finally opened.

'Shall I bring Madame Steuvels in at the same time?' Liotard asked.

Fernande had been crying and was holding her handkerchief in her hand. Immediately, she turned to Maigret and threw him a look of distress, as if she was still expecting him to sort things out.

Steuvels hadn't changed. He still had that mild yet stubborn look of his, and he went and sat down meekly on the chair to which he was motioned.

When the clerk tried to take his seat, Judge Dossin said, 'Later. I'll call you when the interrogation becomes official. Do you agree, Maître Liotard?'

'Absolutely. Thank you.'

Only Maigret was still standing facing the window, down which droplets of rain were falling. The Seine was as grey as the sky, and the barges, the roofs and the pavements all glistened with wetness.

Then Judge Dossin coughed two or three times and said hesitantly, 'I think, Monsieur Steuvels, that the detective chief inspector would like to ask you a few questions.'

Maigret, who had just lit his pipe, was forced to turn, attempting as he did so to wipe an amused smile from his face.

'I assume,' he began, still standing, with the air of teaching a class, 'that your defence counsel has brought you up to date? We know what you and your brother were up to. As far as you personally are concerned, we may have nothing else against you.

'The fact is, the bloodstained suit wasn't yours, it was your brother's. He left his in your house and took yours away with him.'

'My brother didn't kill anyone either.'

'That may be so. Do you want me to question you, or would you prefer to tell us what you know?'

Not only did he now have an ally in Maître Liotard, but Fernande was looking beseechingly at Frans, encouraging him to speak.

'Question me. I'll see if I can answer.'

He wiped his thick glasses and waited, shoulders rounded, head bent forward a little as if it were too heavy.

'When did you find out that the Countess Panetti had been killed?'

'On the Saturday night.'

'You mean the night Moss, Levine and a third person who was probably Krynker came to see you?'

'Yes.'

'Was it you who thought of having a telegram sent to your wife to get her out of the house?'

'I didn't know anything about it.'

That was plausible. Alfred Moss knew enough about the habits of the household and the couple's lifestyle.

'So when you heard a knock at your door at about nine in the evening, you had no idea who it was?'

'That's right. In fact I didn't want to let them in. I was reading peacefully in the basement.'

'What did your brother tell you?'

'That one of the people with him needed a passport that same evening, that he had brought what was required, and that I had to get to work immediately.'

'Was it the first time he'd brought strangers to your house?'

'He knew I didn't want to see anyone.'

'But you knew he had accomplices?'

'He told me he worked with someone named Schwartz.'

'The man who went under the name Levine in Rue Lepic? Quite a fat man, dark-skinned?'

'Yes.'

'Did you all go down to the basement?'

'Yes. I couldn't do anything in the workshop at that hour. The neighbours would have been suspicious.'

'Tell me about the third man.'

'I don't know him.'

'Did he have a foreign accent?'

'Yes. He was Hungarian. He seemed anxious to leave and insisted on knowing he wouldn't get into any trouble with a false passport.'

'For what country?'

'The United States. They're the most difficult to imitate, because of certain special marks known only to consulates and the immigration services.'

'Did you start work on it?'

'I didn't have time.'

'What happened?'

'Schwartz was walking around the apartment, as if to make sure we couldn't be caught by surprise. All of a sudden, when I had my back turned – I was leaning over the suitcase, which had been placed on a chair – I heard a gunshot and saw the Hungarian collapse.'

'Was it Schwartz who'd fired?'

'Yes.'

'Did your brother seem surprised?'

A second's hesitation. 'Yes.'

'What happened next?'

'Schwartz told us it was the only possible solution and he had no choice. He said Krynker was in too nervous a state and was bound to get caught. And when that happened, he'd talk.

'"I was wrong to think he was a man," he added.

'Then he asked me where the stove was.'

'He knew there was one?'

'I think so.'

Through Moss, obviously, just as it was obvious that Frans didn't want to incriminate his brother.

'He ordered Alfred to light the stove, and asked me to bring the sharpest tools I had.

'"We're all in the same boat, my friends. If I hadn't killed this idiot, we would have been arrested within the week. Nobody's seen him with us. Nobody knows he's here. He has no family to ask after him. Get rid of him and we're safe."'

Now wasn't the moment to ask Steuvels if they had all helped in cutting up the body.

'Did he tell you about the death of the old woman?'

'Yes.'

'Was it the first time you'd heard about it?'

'I hadn't seen anybody since they'd all gone off in the car.'

He was becoming more reluctant to speak. Fernande kept looking from her husband to Maigret.

'Out with it, Frans. They got you into this and then ran away. What's the point of keeping quiet?'

'As your defence lawyer,' Maître Liotard chimed in, 'I can tell you it's not only your duty to speak, but in your own best interests. I think the law will applaud you for your honesty.'

Frans looked at him, his big eyes blurry now, and gave a slight shrug. 'They spent most of the night there,' he said at last. 'It took a long time.'

Fernande raised her handkerchief to her mouth to stop herself retching.

'Schwartz, or Levine, or whatever his name was, had a bottle of brandy in his coat pocket, and my brother drank a lot.

'At one point, Schwartz lost his temper and said, "This is the second time you've done this to me!"

'And that was when Alfred told me about the old woman.'

'Just a moment,' Maigret cut in. 'What exactly do you know about Schwartz?'

'That he's the man my brother was working for. He'd told me about him a number of times. He said he was very good, but dangerous. He has a child by a pretty Italian girl he lives with most of the time.'

'Gloria?'

'Yes. Schwartz worked mainly in grand hotels. He'd

spotted a rich, eccentric old woman he thought he could get something from, and he'd persuaded Gloria to work for her.'

'And Krynker?'

'I only ever really saw him dead. He'd only been there for a few moments when he was shot. There are some things I only realized later, when I thought about it.'

'For example?'

'That Schwartz had carefully planned it all. He wanted to get rid of Krynker and he'd found a way to do it without running any risks. He knew what was going to happen when he came to my place. He'd sent Gloria to Concarneau to send the telegram to Fernande.'

'What about the old woman?'

'I wasn't involved in any of that. All I know is that since his divorce, Krynker, who spent time on the Riviera, had been trying to get close to her. Lately, he'd actually succeeded, and she sometimes gave him little sums of money. It soon got frittered away, because he liked to live the high life. What he wanted was enough money to go to the United States.'

'Did he still love his wife?'

'I don't know. He made the acquaintance of Schwartz, or rather Schwartz, who'd been alerted by Gloria, arranged things so that they met in a bar, and they got quite friendly.'

'And it was on the night Krynker died and ended up in the stove that they told you all this?'

'We had to wait several hours for . . .'

'I understand.'

'I wasn't told if the idea was Krynker's or if Schwartz suggested it to him. The old woman was apparently in the habit of travelling with a little case that contained a fortune in jewellery.

'It was just about the season when she went every year to the Riviera. They just had to persuade her to leave in Krynker's car.

'On the way, at a given moment, the car would be attacked and the case would be taken.

'In Krynker's mind, it was supposed to happen without bloodshed. He was convinced he wasn't running any risk, because he'd be in the car with his former mother-in-law.

'For some reason, Schwartz fired, and I think he did it deliberately. It was a way for him to have the others at his mercy.'

'Including your brother?'

'Yes. The attack took place on the road to Fontainebleau, after which they went to Lagny to get rid of the car. Schwartz had once lived around there and knew the area. What else do you want to know?'

'Where are the jewels?'

'They found the case, but the jewels weren't in it. I guess the countess must have been suspicious after all. Gloria had no idea either, even though she'd worked for her. Maybe she'd deposited them in a bank.'

'That was when Krynker panicked.'

'His first idea was to cross the border, with his real papers, but Schwartz told him he'd be arrested. He couldn't sleep, started drinking a lot. He was beginning to panic, and Schwartz decided that the only way to keep things quiet was to get rid of him. He brought him to me on the pretext of getting him a false passport.'

'How is it that your brother's suit . . .'

'I know what you mean. In the middle of it all, Alfred slipped, just where . . .'

'So you gave him your blue suit, and you kept his and cleaned it the next day?'

Fernande's head must have been full of blood-soaked images. She was looking at her husband as if seeing him for the first time, no doubt trying to imagine him during the days and nights he had subsequently spent alone in the basement and the workshop.

Maigret saw her shudder, but a moment later she hesitantly reached out a hand, which came to rest on Steuvels' big hand.

'Maybe they have a bookbinding workshop in prison,' she murmured, making an effort to smile.

Levine, whose real name was neither Schwartz, nor Levine, but Sarkistian, and who was wanted by the prosecutor's departments of three countries, was arrested a month later in a little village just outside Orléans, where he had been spending his time fishing.

Two days later, Gloria Lotti was found in a brothel in Orléans. She always refused to reveal the names of the country people to whom she had entrusted her son.

As for Alfred Moss, his description remained in the police bulletins for four years.

One night, a seedy clown hanged himself in a little circus that travelled from village to village in the North, and it was when the local gendarmes examined the papers found in his suitcase that they learned his identity.

The Countess Panetti's jewels hadn't left Claridge's – they were still in one of the trunks she had deposited there – and the cobbler in Rue de Turenne never admitted, even when he was dead drunk, that he had written the anonymous letter.

OTHER TITLES IN THE SERIES

THE JUDGE'S HOUSE
GEORGES SIMENON

'He went out, lit his pipe and walked slowly to the harbour. He could hear scurrying footsteps behind him. The sea was becoming swollen. The beams of the lighthouses joined in the sky. The moon had just risen and the judge's house emerged from the darkness, all white, a crude, livid, unreal white.'

Exiled from the Police Judiciare in Paris, Maigret bides his time in a remote coastal town in France. There, among the lighthouses, mussel farms and the eerie wail of foghorns, he discovers that a community's loyalties hide unpleasant truths.

Translated by Howard Curtis

INSPECTOR MAIGRET

OTHER TITLES IN THE SERIES

SIGNED, PICPUS
GEORGES SIMENON

'"It's a matter of life and death!" he said.

A small, thin man, rather dull to look at, neither young nor old, exuding the stale smell of a bachelor who does not look after himself. He pulls his fingers and cracks his knuckles while telling his tale, the way a schoolboy recites his lesson.'

A mysterious note predicting the murder of a fortune-teller; a confused old man locked in a Paris apartment; a financier who goes fishing; a South American heiress... Maigret must make his way through a frustrating maze of clues, suspects and motives to find out what connects them.

Translated by David Coward

OTHER TITLES IN THE SERIES

INSPECTOR CADAVER
GEORGES SIMENON

'To everyone, even the old ladies hiding behind their quivering curtains, even the kids just now who had turned to stare after they had passed him, he was the intruder, the undesirable.'

Asked to help a friend in trouble, Maigret arrives in a small provincial town where curtains twitch and gossip is rife. He also finds himself facing an unexpected adversary: the pale, shifty ex-policeman they call 'Inspector Cadaver'.

Translated by William Hobson

INSPECTOR MAIGRET

OTHER TITLES IN THE SERIES

FÉLICIE
GEORGES SIMENON

'In his mind's eye he would see that slim figure in the striking clothes, those wide eyes the colour of forget-me-not, the pert nose and especially the hat, that giddy, crimson bonnet perched on the top of her head with a bronze-green feather shaped like a blade stuck in it.'

Investigating the death of a retired sailor on the outskirts of Paris, Maigret meets his match in the form of the old man's housekeeper: the sharp-witted, enigmatic and elusive Félicie.

Translated by David Coward

OTHER TITLES IN THE SERIES